COUNTRY
LEGACY

COUNTRY LEGACY

A MAVERICK TO (RE)MARRY

NEW YORK TIMES BESTSELLING AUTHOR

Christine Rimmer

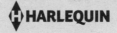

Special thanks and acknowledgment are given to
Christine Rimmer for her contribution to the
Montana Mavericks: The Lonelyhearts Ranch continuity.

Recycling programs
for this product may
not exist in your area.

ISBN-13: 978-1-335-52347-1

A Maverick to (Re)Marry
First published in 2018. This edition published in 2022.
Copyright © 2018 by Harlequin Enterprises ULC

For questions and comments about the quality of this book,
please contact us at CustomerService@Harlequin.com.

Harlequin Enterprises ULC
22 Adelaide St. West, 41st Floor
Toronto, Ontario M5H 4E3, Canada
www.Harlequin.com

Printed in U.S.A.

Christine Rimmer came to her profession the long way around. She tried everything from acting to teaching to telephone sales. Now she's finally found work that suits her perfectly. She insists she never had a problem keeping a job—she was merely gaining "life experience" for her future as a novelist. Christine lives with her family in Oregon. Visit her at christinerimmer.com.

For everyone who's loved and lost
and dared to try again.

Chapter 1

"I can't believe you're here at last," said Eva Rose Armstrong with a tender little smile. "When you pulled up in your fancy car yesterday, I almost wondered if I was seeing things."

"I'm here and I'm staying," Amy Wainwright replied. "You won't get rid of me until the wedding, no matter how hard you try," she spoke firmly and did her best to ignore the growing sense of dread that had her stomach feeling queasy and her nerves on a thin edge.

"Thirteen years," Eva scolded fondly, "do you realize that? Thirteen years it's taken us to get you to come back to town." *Us* included Eva and her older sisters, Delphine and Calla. Growing up, the Armstrong sisters had been like family to Amy. In the years since Amy had moved to Colorado, the Armstrong girls had come to visit her often, but Amy had always found some reason she couldn't make the trip to Rust Creek Falls—and in actual fact, it had been nine years, not thirteen, since Amy had last set foot in Montana. But Eva didn't know about that other visit and she never would.

"It took you getting married to do the trick." Amy strove for a light tone. "But I'm here now. And I'm going nowhere until I see you walk down the aisle to the man that you love."

Eva laughed. "You don't have to look so grim and determined about it."

Relax, Amy reminded herself for the umpteenth time. *It's going to be fine.* "Grim?" She reached out and took Eva's hand. "Are you kidding? I'm thrilled to be your maid of honor." It was coming face-to-face again with the best man that had her belly in knots and her heart stuck in her throat.

They stood near the sunny front window in the living room of the farmhouse where Eva lived with her fiancé, Luke Stockton. The best man would be joining them any minute now. And Amy would get through this meeting with her pride and her dignity intact.

She was going to smile in a cordial sort of way, just smile and say hello and ask him how he'd been. She would treat him as exactly what he was—a guy she knew way back when. An old high school boyfriend, nothing more.

What had really happened between them all those years ago was their secret, his and hers. And Amy could see no reason on earth why it shouldn't stay that way.

"Now, we just need to find a way to keep you here forever," Eva said with a definite smirk.

"Highly unlikely." Amy lived in Boulder. She owned her own home and she worked for a major accounting firm as a digital forensic accountant. Most people's eyes glazed over when she talked about her work, but Amy had always been a math whiz and a computer nerd. She totally loved stopping hackers and fraudsters dead in their tracks.

"You never know," Eva teased, "you could finally meet the man of your dreams right here in Rust Creek Falls. This town is magic when it comes to love and romance, you just ask anyone."

Once, long ago, Amy would have agreed with her friend. Now, though? Not happening. No way, uh-uh. "If you say so…"

Eva tugged on her hand. "Come on." She led Amy to the sofa and chairs grouped around the coffee table. Eva and Luke had moved to Sunshine Farm last winter. Slowly, they'd been fixing up the old farmhouse, stripping dated wallpaper, installing new countertops and appliances in the kitchen. The furniture was mostly family hand-me-downs and stuff picked up at estate and yard sales, but Eva had a great sense of style and the effect was homey. Welcoming. "Sit down," Eva said, "and have a cookie."

Amy took one of the two wing chairs across from the couch—and a lemon-praline macaron. Eva was a baker by profession, her cookies as irresistible as her sunny smile.

The doorbell chimed.

It's him...

Adrenaline spurted. Amy's throat locked up tight on a bite of macaron.

Calm down. You're okay. Breathe. She gulped a sip of iced tea and somehow managed to swallow the bite of cookie without surrendering to a choking fit.

Across the room and through the open arch, in the small foyer, Eva pulled open the door. "Viv!" It was the wedding planner, Vivienne Shuster. Not *him*, after all. Amy's heartbeat slowed a little as Eva ushered the other woman into the living room.

Vivienne, a tall, striking blonde in a simple tan skirt and a white shirt, took a seat on the couch. She set down her stack of pastel binders and her tablet, shook hands with Amy and said yes to a glass of iced tea and a butter-pecan sandy.

For a few minutes, the women chatted about nothing in particular. Viv was relatively new to town, just getting started with her wedding-planner business. "Eva, the house looks great."

"We keep working on it," said Eva. Luke had grown up at Sunshine Farm, but the place had fallen into disrepair when his parents died and the Stockton family was torn apart.

Viv had obviously heard the whole heart-breaking story, including the current state of affairs. "It's wonderful," she said, "that Luke and his brothers and sisters are reunited now— or almost." Her bright smile dimmed a little. "Any word on Liza?" Liza Stockton was the only one of Luke's siblings who had yet to be located.

"No. But we're still looking. We'll never give up."

"Well, you're certainly bringing the family ranch back to life again." Viv picked up one of her binders and flipped to a tab labeled *Barn Weddings*. Like Luke's brother Danny last Christmas, Luke and Eva's wedding venue would be the big yellow barn right there on Sunshine Farm. "So, we're still going with holding the ceremony outside, and then the reception dinner in the barn, right?" At Eva's nod, Viv continued, "Good, then. I have a few new ideas to run by you."

Amy heard boots out on the front steps. Her mouth went dust-dry and her ears started ringing.

But it was only Luke coming in from the horse pasture. She took slow, deep breaths to settle her absurdly overactive nerves as Luke left his muddy boots by the door and slipped on a pair of soft mocs. "Am I late?"

"Nope." Eva got up to offer a quick kiss and pull him into the living room. "You're right on time." *They look so happy together*, Amy thought. She was glad for her friend. A born romantic, Eva had survived more than her share of disappointments in love. But she never gave up. And now she'd finally found the perfect man for her.

The doorbell rang again. Amy's stomach lurched and her heart beat so hard, she knew it would pound its way right out of her chest.

"That'll be Derek," Luke said. "I'll get it." He returned to the door as Amy practiced slow breathing and prayed she wouldn't sink to the floor in a dead faint like the heroine of some old-time novel, felled by her own secret past. "Come on in," said Luke.

And then, there he was.

Derek Dalton. In Wranglers and a soft chambray shirt. He took off his hat and his hair was just as she remembered it, thick and unruly, sable brown. *He* was just as she remembered— only bigger, broader. A grown man now, not a nineteen-year-old boy.

He hung his hat by the door. Luke signaled him forward and he entered the living room, filling it with his presence, with their past that seemed to suck all the air right out of her lungs. He greeted Eva and Viv. And then he turned to Amy, those leaf-green eyes homing right in on her. "Hey, Amy. Long time, huh?"

She stared up at him, unable to speak. But then he held out his big, blunt-fingered, work-roughened hand. She forced herself to take it and the shock of touching him again after all these years sent a bolt of lightning straight up her arm—and jolted the necessary words out of her.

"Hey, Derek." She pulled her fingers free

of his grip and somehow managed the barest semblance of a smile. "Great to see you again."

"You, too." With that, he turned away at last and lowered his big frame into the other wing chair.

The meeting began.

Viv opened a binder, pulled the rings wide and took out a small stack of papers. "Derek." She handed several sheets to him. "And for you, Amy." She passed Amy the rest. "You each now have the phone numbers and email addresses of everyone in the wedding party. Also, you'll find a series of suggestions for the joint bachelor-bachelorette party, which is slated for the Saturday before the wedding. You two will be working as a team to pull it together. Invitations have already been sent and we're counting on a big crowd. I threw in a few brainstorming sheets. It always helps to have those—just as a way to get the ideas flowing, you understand."

"Wonderful," Amy said, because Viv was looking at her and it seemed important that she say something.

"As for the bachelor party venue," said Viv, "Maverick Manor is a dream setting, luxe and rustic at once. A real coup that we got it." She gave Derek a nod. "Big thanks to Derek."

"Don't thank me," Derek said. His voice was a little different somehow, deeper than Amy remembered. The sound of it reached down inside her, stirring up memories, reminding her of tender moments she really needed to forget. He added, "Nate Crawford's the one."

Eva asked, "You remember Nate, Amy?"

"Yeah. Of course." Nate had been four or five years ahead of her in school, but everybody knew him. He was the oldest of six children. His parents, Laura and Todd, owned the general store.

"Nate's become kind of a town benefactor in the last few years," said Eva. "He's a major shareholder in Maverick Manor."

Derek said, "I just mentioned the party to him and he offered the Manor as a good place for it."

"Ah," said Amy, staring straight ahead, unable to make herself look at him though he was sitting right there at the other end of the coffee table from her. "Terrific."

Eva explained, "Instead of separating the girls and the guys, I wanted one big party for all of us—with nothing X-rated, if you know what I mean."

Viv clarified, "No strippers. And the games can be a *little* sexy—"

"—but nothing over the top." Eva patted Luke's hand. "Just good fun, right, Luke?"

"Works for me." The groom nodded.

"It'll be a nice, relaxed get-together for everyone," added Eva, "not only for the wedding party, but also for all of our friends in town. We want it to be loose and easy and the Manor is a beautiful, comfortable place for it."

Viv nodded at Derek and then at Amy. "Food and music are already taken care of, again thanks to Derek."

Wait a minute. Had Derek paid for all this? Or just arranged everything? The boy she'd known in high school hadn't had a lot of money. So then, he'd done well for himself?

Not that it mattered how much money he had. What mattered was that she would make sure the financial burden didn't all fall on him—and wait a minute. Why was she worrying about Derek and his finances anyway?

Really, she didn't even know the guy anymore....

Viv was still talking. "If you need specific songs played or whatever, I'll be happy to pass your requests along to the band. You two will be putting your heads together and coming up with some fun things to do for the event, along with party favors and prizes.

"Mostly, it's a balance. You don't want to pack in too many activities, but you need a few games and such, to get people mingling. I've listed some very basic ideas on your party brainstorm sheets, just to jump-start the process for you. I'll be ready with more suggestions if you need them and to help in any way I can."

Amy tried really hard to focus, to keep her mind in the now, to think about great things to do at a coed bachelor party and what prizes and favors might be cute.

But her brain defied her will. Images assailed her, of those five days all those years ago, the tacky motel by the highway, the sound of the big rigs going by in the night, the reassuring warmth of Derek's strong arms around her. How much she had loved him.

How scared she'd been, her life spinning out of control, nothing going the way she'd planned it.

"Fun activities," she heard herself repeat. "Will do."

From the other chair, Derek spoke up, too. "Uh, yeah. We'll get right on that."

The meeting continued. To Amy, it seemed endless. The memories pressed in on her, making it hard to breathe. But really, no one seemed to notice that she wasn't saying much. Did they?

Eva and Luke seemed relaxed, happy as only two people in love can be. Viv was laser-focused on the wedding plans. Eva, a baker to the core, was all about the food and the cake, while Viv talked flowers and ways to make the barn setting really pop.

They discussed music for the wedding day, too. Luke and Eva had put in hours practicing their first dance. The band—the same group they were using at the bachelor party—had been given a long playlist of the couple's favorites to fill up the evening. Luke joked that of course local eccentric Homer Gilmore would be welcome at the wedding. But they had to make absolutely certain that Homer's infamous moonshine didn't find its way into the punch.

As for Derek...

Well, Amy didn't know how Derek was faring. From the moment he took the chair across from hers, she hadn't been able to make herself so much as glance in his direction.

When it was finally over and Viv was closing up her binders and stacking them to go, Amy longed to race for the stairs and the big guest room up there that would be hers for the next few weeks. She'd brought her work with her. She could power up her computer and concentrate on keeping the giant accounting firm of Hurdly and Main, International protected from cyber-criminals and digital fraud.

But no. She and Derek needed to talk.

She needed to tell him…what? There was nothing *to* tell him. It was over and it had been over for years and years.

Still. They really ought to come to some sort of understanding as to how they were going to work together. Not to mention, she needed to know who in town knew about them. And how much they knew. And, from now on, what would be getting said to whom.

Suddenly, everyone was standing and moving toward the door—everyone but Amy. She shook herself and leapt to her feet.

And then once she was up, she just stood there at her chair, dithering over how to approach him, what to say to get his attention before hc went out the door and she missed her chance to tell him…

What?

Dear Lord, she had no idea.

She blinked and finally made herself glance in his direction.

He was looking straight at her. "So, Amy, got a few minutes?" Those green eyes gave nothing away. "We should touch base."

Her heart pounding so hard she was lucky

it didn't crack a rib, she nodded. "A walk, maybe?" she heard herself offer lamely.

"That'll work."

It took her several agonizing seconds to realize that he was waiting for her to join him. "Oh!" she exclaimed like a total doofus and ordered her feet to carry her toward him.

They all went out to the porch together and waved goodbye to Viv.

Luke shook Derek's hand. "Friday, happy hour. The Ace."

"I'll be there," said Derek.

The Ace in the Hole was the only bar within the Rust Creek Falls town limits. Amy remembered it all too well from her short, unhappy visit to town nine years before.

And then, last year, the Ace had garnered national attention when a reality show, *The Great Roundup*, had filmed final auditions there. Travis Dalton, Derek's cousin, had been on that show and so had Travis's now-wife, Brenna O'Reilly Dalton.

Amy had watched the show faithfully every week. The scenes filmed in town had made her feel all warm and fuzzy, made her long for Rust Creek Falls, made her remember the good times growing up. Best of all, *The Great Roundup* had allowed her to get sappy and sentimental from the safety of her Boulder, Colorado living room. Never had she ever planned to set foot in town again.

But now, here she was, about to get up close and conversational with the very reason she'd stayed away for so long in the first place.

Luke and Eva went back into the house, leaving Amy alone with the gorgeous broad-shouldered stranger who'd once ruled her teenaged heart. She just stood there, like a lump. She had no idea what to say to him.

He had his straw Resistol in his hand. He slid the hat onto his head and tugged on the brim to settle it.

Everything inside her was aching. This couldn't be happening.

But it was.

"Let's go." He started walking. She followed him down the steps and out into the late-afternoon sunshine.

He turned for the big yellow barn where Eva and Luke would get married in less than four weeks. Amy came up beside him and they walked together, but not touching, neither saying a word. Somewhere far off, a lone bird cried, the sound faint. Plaintive.

"Here's as good as anywhere, I guess," he

said, stopping at a split rail fence fifty yards or so from the looming shape of the barn.

For more reasons than she cared to contemplate, she didn't want to look directly at him, so she turned toward the pasture on the other side of the fence. The papers Viv had given her crackled in her hands as she rested her forearms on the top rail and gazed off at nothing in particular.

Silence. Out in the pasture, a bay mare snorted and shook her dark mane.

Derek said, "You look good," and she tried to read his tone. Careful? Thoughtful? Maybe a little angry?

What did it matter, though, what was on his mind? She didn't know him anymore. They were strangers to each other now and she needed to remember that. "Thanks. You, too—and, well, I don't even know where to start." She did look at him then. He was watching her from under the shadow of his hat. Waiting. She swallowed. Hard. "I have been wondering, though…"

"What?"

"Well, it would be good to have some idea of who *knows*," she said, and then wanted to kick herself. Could she *be* any more unclear? He probably had no clue what she'd just tried to ask him.

But as it turned out, he understood perfectly. "About us, you mean?"

"Yeah. About, um, what happened thirteen years ago."

"Nobody in this town," he said. "Nobody but me." A slow smile curved his beautiful mouth. "Well, and you, now that you're here. *While* you're here."

She caught her lower lip between her teeth. "I would like it to stay that way."

"Just between you and me, you mean?"

"Yes, Derek." His name in her mouth tasted way too familiar. "Just between us. Can we keep it that way?"

"You got it. I've never told a soul and I won't start now." And then he frowned. "But what about the Armstrongs? You didn't ever tell Eva or her sisters?"

"No." Her silly throat had clutched and the word came out in a whisper. She knew her cheeks had to be lobster-red. "Ahem." She coughed into her hand. And then she made herself explain. "I never told the Armstrongs the whole story. All they know is that you and I dated in high school. How about Luke? Your family?"

"I meant what I said, Amy. I haven't told anyone. It just seemed better to put the whole thing behind me. It's the past and it needs to stay that way."

"I agree." And she did. Absolutely, she did. She wished that none of it had ever happened.

But it did happen. And it changed her in the deepest way.

Did it change him, too, she wondered?

Not that she would ever ask. She had no right to ask and she needed to remember that.

He smiled again—halfway this time, one corner of his mouth kicking up. "Luke waited until after I said I would be his best man to tell me that you would be the maid of honor."

A strange, tight spurt of laughter escaped her. She quickly composed herself. "I see Eva all over that."

"What do you mean?"

"She got me to agree to be her maid of honor before she mentioned that you would be best man."

"So, you think she knows more than you've told her?"

"Well, you know Eva, right? She's a complete and unapologetic romantic. I think she suspects there was more than just a high school crush going on between us back in the day." Another tight little laugh escaped her—and then she wanted to cry. Really, she couldn't stand for him not to know what she truly felt, how much she regretted the way things had ended up. "Derek, I…"

"Yeah?" His eyes held hers, a deep look, one that reached down into the center of her and stirred up emotions she wished she didn't feel.

"I, well, I just need you to know that I'm sorry. For everything."

Wow. She almost couldn't believe that she'd gone and done it, apologized straight out. And as soon as the words escaped her lips, she kind of wanted to take them back.

Because really, wasn't *he* the one who'd told *her* to go?

But what else could a person say at a time like this?

"I'm sorry, too," he said.

"But it's fine," she blurted out.

He nodded. "Yeah. You're right. It's water under the bridge. Years ago. Not a big deal."

"Absolutely. Over and done. We've both put it behind us. Derek, we can do this. We can be there for Luke and Eva. We can help make their wedding everything they deserve it to be."

He took off his hat, hit the brim against his denim-clad thigh, then put it back on. "Yeah. That's our job and we can do it."

She straightened her shoulders. "We *will* do it."

"Yes, we will," he agreed.

And then they just stood there at the fence, staring at each other.

The silence stretched thin.

He broke it. "Well, all right, then. I'll be in touch." And without another word, he turned and left her standing there.

Chapter 2

Feeling stunned by the whole encounter, Amy stared after Derek as he walked away from her.

Once he reached the turnaround in front of the house again, he climbed into a mud-spattered red F-150 pickup. The engine roared out, the big wheels stirring up a cloud of dust as he drove away.

What had just happened? She wasn't sure. Had they actually forgiven each other?

Well, at least they'd said the words. And that was good, she decided. They didn't need to talk it to death. What was there to say, anyway?

It was all in the past.

Too bad they'd come up with nothing in

terms of a plan for the bachelor party. He'd said he would "be in touch." What exactly did that mean?

Annoyance prickled through her. Okay, she got that she wasn't his favorite person. But they did have to work together. He could have stuck around long enough to set a time and a place.

She glanced down at the papers in her hand. His numbers were right there at the top of the first page—mobile and home. Would the home number be the main house at his family's ranch, the Circle D? She'd had that number memorized all those years ago. It was burned into her brain and she remembered it still. But this home number was different. Did he live somewhere else now?

He'd moved to the bunkhouse in April of their senior year, to give himself a little independence from his close-knit family. Back then, the bunkhouse number was the same as at the main house, but maybe they'd put in a separate line since then.

Not that she cared. It didn't matter to her where, exactly, he lived now. She just needed to know when and where they would meet.

She shook her head at the stack of papers. If he didn't get back to her in the next day or two, she would have to call him.

No big deal.

And really, he *had* said he would be in touch, right? What was she worrying about?

Forget calling him. *He* would call *her*.

And of course, that would be soon...

Amy barely got back in the door of the farmhouse before Eva was all over her. "What did he say? Is it okay between you? Was it hard, to see him again?"

"Eva." She managed a laugh. "Cut it out. It was fine. It was years ago."

"But you *loved* him."

Oh, yes, she had. But she wasn't going there. "It was high school. And it's all in the past. There are no problems between us and you don't have to worry."

"I'm not worrying." Her big blue eyes got bigger. "I just want to know, is the spark still there?"

Amy wasn't answering that one. No way. She kept it light, making a show of tapping her chin as though deep in thought. "Hmm. Is it just me or are you playing matchmaker?"

Eva blushed the sweetest shade of pink. "I would never..."

"Yeah, right."

They both burst out laughing at the same

time and Eva said, "Okay, okay. I'll butt out, I promise."

Amy gave her friend the side-eye. "I'll believe it when I see it."

Derek didn't call that evening. And he didn't call on Tuesday.

By Wednesday, the Fourth of July, she knew she should go ahead and reach out.

Maybe a text. She wouldn't even have to talk to him until their actual meeting.

She put his cell number in her phone, hit the message icon and started typing, whipping out five different messages and deleting them as fast as she wrote them. After the fifth attempt, she decided she would just wait another day to deal with the whole reaching out thing.

That night, she went into town with Eva, Luke and his brother Bailey, for a barbecue at their sister Bella's house and to watch the fireworks in the town park later. That whole evening, she felt on edge just thinking that she might run into Derek.

But she never so much as caught sight of him.

The days were going by. They needed to meet up. But he hadn't called.

And she couldn't quite bring herself to make the first move.

* * *

By Thursday evening, as he ate his solitary dinner in the house he'd built for himself on Circle D land, Derek Dalton was feeling more than a little bit jerkish.

He'd told Amy he would get back to her. He needed to call her and set up another meeting.

But even after all these years, it still hurt something deep inside him just to be near her. She looked the same—with long brown hair showing gleams of red in the sun, creamy skin, eyes that seemed to change color depending on her mood, brown to olive green and back again, sometimes with a hint of gold.

Yeah. She looked the same. But even better, so smooth and classy. Luke had mentioned that she'd gone on to graduate school after four years at the University of Colorado. He'd said she had some high-tech accounting job and she owned her own house in Boulder.

None of that information surprised Derek. Amy had been the smartest girl at Rust Creek Falls High, put ahead a year when she was twelve, so they'd ended up in the same grade. She'd been valedictorian of their small graduating class. Her dad was a rich guy from Boulder who'd given up the rat race for a while to become a rancher in the Rust Creek Falls Valley—and then moved back to Colorado when Amy left to go to college there.

Derek never would've had a chance with Jack and Helen Wainwright's precious only daughter if he hadn't needed a math tutor to get him through Algebra II in his senior year.

He shook his head. Him and Amy? That was an old, sad song and they wouldn't be playing it ever again. He needed to get his mind off the past. There was zero to be gained by a trip down memory lane.

Shoving back his chair, he picked up his plate and carried it to the counter. Outside the window over the sink, the sunset turned the bellies of the clouds to bright orange and deep purple.

Maybe he'd head on into town, see if he could scare up a poker game at the Ace.

Then again, he'd had a long day today, moving cattle, putting out mineral barrels. Tomorrow, he needed to be up early. He felt antsy and ornery. If he went to the Ace, it would be too easy to drink too much and do or say something he would end up regretting.

He turned in early and had a restless night.

But it could have been worse. At least he didn't have a hangover at eight on Friday morning when he parked his pickup in front of the old warehouse at Sawmill and North Broomtail Road.

Four years ago, he'd joined Collin Traub in his one-man saddlery business. At first, they'd worked in the basement of Collin's house up on Falls Mountain. But then CT Saddles had moved to the warehouse. The larger space allowed them to buy more equipment and take on more projects. They were still a small shop, but the Traub name was a trusted one and their business kept growing.

Derek thought about Amy constantly that day. Really, it was way past time he gave her a call. But the hours ticked by and he never did.

His failure to get back to her was moving beyond jerkish, heading into jackass territory. But he still failed to pick up the phone.

At five, Collin went on up the mountain to his wife, Willa, and their little boy, Robbie. Ned Faraday, who was sixteen and helping out at the saddlery for the summer, headed home for dinner.

Derek washed up in the saddlery restroom and thought again about how he needed to call Amy. He even took out his phone and looked at it for a good minute or two before shaking his head and sticking it back in his pocket.

At five thirty, he walked down the street to the Ace to meet Luke and his brothers for a drink. It was the five of them—Luke, Jamie, Daniel, Bailey and Derek. They took over a big table not far from the bar and ordered some pitchers.

Jamie and Daniel Stockton were both happily married. Jamie had triplets, Henry, Jared and Kate. They were two and a half years old now. Jamie got everyone laughing with stories of the mischief the three little ones got up to. Danny spoke fondly of his wife and their daughter, Janie.

And Luke? He mostly just sat there, slowly sipping his beer with a contented smile on his face. Everyone in town knew that Luke Stockton was long-gone in love with Eva Rose Armstrong and couldn't wait to make her his wife.

Bailey was the lone unattached Stockton brother. He'd been married and divorced. Like Luke and Daniel, he'd returned to town in the past year after more than a decade away. Now he lived at Sunshine Farm. He and Luke worked the ranch together, building a new herd, bringing the family homestead back from years of neglect.

That evening, Bailey didn't say much at first. But after a beer or two, he started making his feelings about matrimony painfully clear.

"It's a losin' game is what it is." He raised his glass to Derek, who'd taken the chair across from him. "And you, my man, are the only one at this table with the sense the good Lord gave a goat.

You got the ladies all over you, but no woman ever tied *you* down and slapped on a brand."

Ignoring the sudden sweet image of Amy that popped into his head unbidden, Derek forced a wry laugh. "Put a sock in it, Bailey. Your brothers look pretty damn happy to me."

Bailey groaned. "They all start out happy, now don't they?"

"You're getting obnoxious," warned Luke. "Quit while you're ahead."

But Bailey wasn't about to take his brother's good advice. "What I'm 'getting' is honest. It's too late for Danny and Jamie here. They'll just have to learn the hard way that marriage is a game for fools." He leaned close to Luke and stage-whispered in his ear, "Get away. Get away while you still can."

"Knock it off." Luke elbowed him hard in the ribs.

"Ow!" Bailey rubbed his side. "Big brother, you got an elbow on you."

"And you have a big mouth. One you need to practice shutting."

Bailey put on a hangdog expression. "It's hopeless, I tell you. You're doomed, brother. Doomed." He tipped his head back and asked the ceiling, "Oh, why won't anyone listen to a man who knows?"

"Get real, Bailey," said Luke. "You love Eva."

"'Course I love Eva. She's a fine woman. So is Annie, for that matter." That was Daniel's wife. "Fallon, too." Fallon O'Reilly had married Jamie the year before. "It's not the women I object to, it's the institution itself. Marriage. It's what ruins people's lives." Bailey wrapped his hands around his own throat and pretended to choke himself. "Slow strangulation, you hear what I'm sayin'?"

Derek decided to step in before Bailey got too far on the wrong side of his own brothers. "Come on, Bailey. Nine-ball. Two out of three." He nodded toward the pool table.

"Go." Daniel made a shooing motion. "Give the rest of us a break."

Bailey scowled. "I'm trying to *help* you."

"We don't need your help," said Jamie.

Bailey hung his head. "Why does no one appreciate the wisdom I'm offering?"

Derek got up. "Nine-ball. What do you say?"

"Why not?" Bailey rose, grumbling, "I'm not makin' any progress here, and that's for sure."

At the pool tables, Bailey continued to trash-talk marriage as Derek proceeded to win the game. Twice.

"Not only smart enough to stay single," declared Bailey when they started back to join the other guys, "but a pool shark, too. What other talents you got?"

As he considered what to try next to get Bailey to stop annoying his brothers, Bailey muttered, "Uh-oh. Here they come."

They were Eva, Bailey's sister Bella—and Amy.

Amy. Looking like a bright ray of sunshine in a pretty yellow dress.

The three women marched straight to the table where the Stockton men were sitting.

Bailey, still beside him, said something else. Derek had no idea what. All rational thought had fled his mind, along with his ability to understand words. He felt sucker punched. And also guilty.

Yeah, he should have called her. But how could he? Even after all these years, she made him forget the English language, made him blind to everything but her.

Somehow, he did what he had to do—put one foot in front of the other, kept walking alongside Bailey until they reached the table again.

"There you are," said Bella, glaring straight at Bailey.

Bailey widened his eyes. "What'd I do now?"

"Don't play innocent," said Bella. "Nobody believes that act from you. You've been driving everybody in the place crazy, going on about all the reasons men should never get married. We just came over to offer you a ride back to Sunshine Farm."

"Somebody called you to come and haul me out of the Ace?" Bailey huffed in trumped-up outrage. "I don't believe this town. A guy can't express an honest opinion without some busybody callin' his sister to come drag him home."

Luke, who'd gotten up to give Eva a quick kiss, advised, "Maybe you've had one too many, huh, Bailey?"

"I'm not drunk," Bailey insisted.

Eva suggested wryly, "Just opinionated?"

He frowned at her. "And where do you and Amy come in? That's what I'd like to know."

"We were over at Bella's when she got the call."

"The call from who?" he demanded.

Bella shook her head. "You don't need to know."

As the others discussed whether Bailey should go home or not, Derek stood by the table and tried not to look at Amy. When he finally couldn't stop himself from shooting her a glance, he caught her at the moment that her gaze skittered away from him.

Just like on Monday, the two of them sitting

there in Eva's living room, both of them trying their damnedest not to look at each other.

They'd had love once, powerful love that
he'd believed could conquer anything.

Now they just tried not to look at each other
when they met up by accident. And when they
had to speak to each other, they blathered on
about how their secret past was long ago and
they were both just fine.

Bailey said, "I'll switch to ginger ale. Will
that satisfy you women?"

"And stop running down marriage," said
Jamie.

"Yeah," Daniel agreed. "We've heard enough
about that."

"Fine, fine. It's hopeless to even try, anyway," Bailey groused. "I got the message, loud
and clear. You all can keep your happily-ever-
afters, see if I care."

"All right, then," said Luke. He turned to Eva.
"Stay for a little?" He sat again and pulled her
down into the chair next to him. "Come on,
Bella. Amy. Stay."

Bailey helped Derek grab some more chairs
and then the two of them went and got another
round—including a pitcher of ginger ale for
Bailey and anyone else who didn't want beer.

When they got back to the table, the chair on one side of Amy was empty.

Derek took that chair because he couldn't bear not to.

Someone put a love song on the ancient juke-box. A girl from out of town grabbed Bailey and pulled him up for a dance.

Luke led Eva out onto the floor. They swayed to the music, whispering to each other. Eva tipped her blond head back and laughed. They looked so damn happy.

Life? Sometimes it just wasn't fair.

Derek couldn't stop himself. He turned to Amy. "Dance with me?"

Her eyes looked almost golden right then, golden, green and softest brown. She swallowed. And then she nodded.

He took her hand—so smooth and cool. It fit just right in his, same as it used to all those years ago. He pulled her up and led her out among the dancers, gathering her close, maybe closer than he should have.

So what? She smelled like heaven—like wildflowers and sunshine. And her body felt just right brushing close to his. Maybe he'd dance with her all night long, never once let her out of his arms.

He pressed his rough cheek to her silky hair. "I'm sorry I didn't call."

"Why didn't you?"

"I don't know. I kept meaning to."

She pulled away enough to turn those big eyes up to him. "Apology accepted. I was going to call *you*."

He stared at her lips too long, caught himself and shifted his glance back up to meet her eyes. "But you didn't call me."

"I didn't know what I would say. I also had a feeling you might not answer the phone or call me back. I felt…out of my depth, I guess. So, I just kept putting it off."

"Yeah, well. All that, what you just said? Me, too."

"We need to stop this. We're two grown adults."

He almost chuckled. "Coulda fooled me."

"Derek, we've got a bachelor party to plan."

He sucked in her scent of flowers and sunshine. "Yeah. We need to get going on that." Holding her like this felt so natural, so completely right. It made the years kind of melt away.

And he really needed to keep a grip on himself. This would go nowhere. It was only a dance.

"So then," she whispered, "we need to make a date to meet and then we need to stick to it."

"A date?" He said it in a playful way and felt stupidly proud of himself that he'd managed to tease her. "You want a date with me?"

She slanted him a sharp glance. "Yeah, a date. But not a *date*."

"So…a *non*-date, then?"

"Exactly. And I mean it, Derek. We need to make it soon. We've got two weeks till the bachelor party. Viv dropped by the farmhouse yesterday and asked how we were doing with our plans. I promised her we'd have it all figured out in the next few days."

Amy was right. No more mooning around like a heartsick fool. It was all over years ago and he needed to stop stewing about it and hold up his end as Luke's best man.

"Tomorrow," he said. "I'll pick you up at six. Ever been to Maverick Manor?"

"No."

"Great. We'll go there and you can get a look at the place. It might give us some ideas."

"All right. That works."

"We'll get a couple of fancy burgers and come up with a bunch of activities to satisfy Viv Shuster's list-making soul."

"Perfect. I'm in."

The song ended.

Another cowboy tapped him on the shoulder. *Get lost*, he almost let himself say. But not quite. He gave Amy a hint of a smile. "Thanks for the dance."

She nodded. "See you tomorrow, then." And she turned into the other cowboy's waiting arms.

The next day, Amy spent way too much time trying to decide what to wear to Maverick Manor that night. She finally settled on a turquoise halter dress with a handkerchief hem and a pair of matching high-heeled sandals. Why not dress up a little? From what everyone said, Maverick Manor was an upscale sort of place.

True, this was not a real date, but it couldn't hurt to look her best.

Maybe, just possibly, she went a little overboard, pumicing and shaving and getting everything all smooth and sleek. And then she used up a whole hour on her hair and makeup. But taking the time to look good was so worth it, a real confidence-booster. And with Derek, well, she needed all the confidence she could muster.

At five thirty, she was trying to decide between a shoulder bag and a clutch, wondering if she ought to bring a light wrap, when her phone rang.

It was Derek. "Amy? Hey. I'm really sorry, but we've got some fences down and I'm not gonna be able to make it tonight, after all. We'll have to reschedule."

Reschedule.

Her heart sank. It felt like a lead weight in her chest.

How had this happened? Somehow, she'd gone and let herself look forward to the evening, let herself forget that this was only a meeting, a *non*-date.

Tears blurred her vision—which was totally ridiculous. She dropped to the edge of her bed and fiddled with the filmy hem of the dress she wouldn't be wearing tonight after all. "Oh. Ahem. Well, I totally understand. You just give me a call tomorrow, why don't you? We'll set up something else."

"Amy, are you all—"

"Listen." She swallowed down the lump in her throat. "I've got to go. Talk to you later."

"But are you—"

"'Bye, now." She disconnected the call and dropped the phone on the bed. And then, teeth gritted, eyes shut, she willed the tears away. So silly, to get all emo just because an old boyfriend needed a rain check on their non-date. It was in no way, shape or form a big deal.

Except, well, he'd been so much more than just a boyfriend…

But she wasn't going to even think about all that. That was all in the past and it needed to stay there. She'd moved on long ago, gone out with other guys. Once, she'd almost gotten engaged. But when it came right down to it, well, it hadn't been true love and she just couldn't say yes. Not like with—

No. Stop. Not going there.

Besides, her dating history was not the issue. What mattered was that the days were flying by and they really did have to make some plans for the big party. They had a great venue and everyone had already been invited. Music and food were taken care of, or so she'd been told.

Games and activities. That was all she and Derek had to handle. And Eva and Luke were counting on them to do it up right.

Really, she would not allow a single tear to fall. Annoyance was what she felt right now. Annoyance and exasperation that Derek Dalton kept putting off the job they'd both agreed to do.

Down the hall in the bathroom, she washed her face free of every bit of the makeup she'd so carefully applied. She raked her hair up into a ponytail and changed into old jeans, a white

T-shirt edged in lace that had seen better days and a worn pair of Converse high-tops.

Then, in her room again, she sat at her computer and spent half an hour brainstorming ideas for the party. When that got old, she logged in at work.

Around eight, she started getting antsy. Grabbing her phone, she went downstairs. Eva and Luke had gone to Jamie and Fallon's for dinner, so she had the house to herself for the evening. She should fix a sandwich or something.

But she didn't really feel hungry.

She wandered out to the front porch and perched on the step. Her phone was synced to her computer. She brought up the list for the party to jot down a few more ideas just as a red pickup rolled into the yard.

Derek. Her pulse started racing and her heart seemed to expand in her chest.

He stopped not far from the foot of the steps and got out. "Hey, pretty girl." He swept off his hat. His hair was damp, his cheeks freshly shaved. He wore dark-wash jeans and a crisp snap-front shirt.

She was really glad to see him and that irritated her no end. Sticking her phone in her back pocket, she challenged, "I thought you had fences to deal with."

"I did. We had three sections of fence down, cows and calves loose all over the place. But we rounded them up and drove them back where they belonged, fixing fences as we went. When we got to the last fence, Eli said he could handle the rest." Eli was his brother. "I left him to it, cleaned up fast and came right over here in hopes I might still have a chance at that non-date you promised me."

She scowled down at her old T-shirt and busted out jeans. "Do I look like I'm ready for a visit to the local resort?"

His gorgeous mouth twitched at one corner. She knew damn well he was trying not to smile. "Aw, Amy."

"What?" she demanded, feeling sour as a pile of lemons.

"You're all grown-up now, but in some ways, you're still the same girl I remember."

Now her chest felt tight, like a bunch of sweet memories had gotten trapped in there, leaving no room for breath. She narrowed her eyes and pinched her mouth at him. "What is *that* supposed to mean?"

"You never would go anywhere without your hair just so and your makeup just right."

She sat up straighter. He wasn't getting to

her. No way. "I like to make a good impression. Something wrong with that?"

"Not a thing." He put his hat to his heart. "I'm sorry, okay? That I didn't call you all week, that tonight got messed up. But when you work cattle, fences go down and you just have to deal with it."

"I know that."

"So then, what's really bugging you is that I didn't call earlier in the week like I said I would?"

She wrapped her arms around her knees, braced her chin on them and considered blowing off his question. But where would that get them? A little honesty never hurt and she might as well at least try to clear the air between them. After all, he'd asked. "Yeah. You said you'd get in touch and you didn't. And then tonight, at the last possible minute, you called it off. It's like you're messing with me or something."

"I'm not."

"And I'm not sure I believe you. I mean, whatever happened in the past, that was then. We need to get over it."

"I know that, Amy." He regarded her solemnly.

"We have a job to do, Derek." Did she sound whiny? Well, why shouldn't she? She certainly *felt* whiny. "People we care about are counting on us."

"You're right." He took a step closer and spoke in a rough whisper. "You want the truth from me?"

Did she? Really? She wasn't sure. But she had too much pride to back down now. "Yes, I do. Tell me the truth, Derek Dalton."

"I didn't call all week because I kept thinking of the past, you know? Of you and me and everything that went down. I didn't trust myself to call you. After everything we were to each other once, I felt like I was going to end up blowing it, saying something way out of line to you. I don't want to do that. And so, I put off calling you."

That hurt. On a lot of levels. But the truth was like that sometimes. "It's not that easy for me, either," she confessed in a small voice.

He stood there in the fading light of day, just looking at her with those green eyes she still sometimes saw in her dreams. "Amy?"

"Yeah?"

"You mind if I come up there on the porch with you?"

By way of an answer, she scooted over and patted the empty space beside her. He came up the steps, hooked his hat on the finial at the end of the porch rail and plunked down next to her. She got a whiff of his scent—soap and clean skin. All manly and fresh and much too well-remembered.

"I…go back and forth," she said.

He frowned. "About?"

She refused to let her gaze waver. "What to say to you. I mean, we did kind of leave it hanging, didn't we?"

His eyes had shadows in them now. "You sent me the papers and I signed them. Nothing left hanging about that."

"Derek, you *told* me to go."

"You *wanted* to go."

She shut her eyes and turned away. "We shouldn't even be talking about this. I mean, what's the point, really?"

There was a silence, one full of all the things she wasn't sure how to say—didn't really believe she even *should* say.

Finally, he spoke. "How 'bout this?" His voice was gentle now. Coaxing. "Let's start with the picnic."

"There's a picnic?" She faced him again. "What picnic?"

"Well, when I called, you didn't seem happy about my breaking our non-date."

"I wasn't happy. Not in the least."

"So, I figured I needed a backup plan. I decided if you wouldn't come out to the Manor with me now, I would put on my pitiful face and say, 'Then how 'bout a picnic, Amy?' Because it just so happens I have one all ready to go in the truck." He looked at her hopefully.

"Is that it?"

"Is what it?"

She waved a hand in a circle around his face. "Is that your pitiful face?"

He chuckled. "It depends. Is it working?"

She was not going to smile at him. He didn't deserve it. Not yet, anyway. "Hmm. Depends on what's in the picnic."

"You'll be relieved to know I stopped by the main house for the food. I have my mom's fried chicken and biscuits all fancy in a basket. I even brought a big blanket to sit on."

"All of a sudden, I'm starving."

"And there's apple pie, too."

She kind of wanted to hold out against him, leave him hanging at least a bit longer. But then her stomach betrayed her with a hungry little growl. His grin said he heard it. At that point, what could she do but give in? "All right. A picnic, then—but I think we'll need to eat inside." She stared out at the darkening sky. "It's almost nighttime. I'm not sure I want to stumble around in the dark looking for somewhere to spread a picnic blanket."

He leaned closer. "Go in and get a sweater. It's getting chilly out."

"But—"

"Shh." His warm breath tickled her ear. "It just so happens I also brought a lantern."

Two hours later, they sat under the stars with the lantern turned down low providing a soft circle of light to push back the shadows.

By then, they'd agreed on the games for the party: a modified version of *The Newlywed Game*, which they'd dubbed "The Nearly Newlywed Game." Also, they planned a scavenger hunt and some random betting and gambling games in a Western-themed, mini-casino setup. They'd made lists of all the things they would need to buy and assemble for each activity, and he'd been fine with her ideas for the decorations.

Tomorrow, she would shop online, making sure to get expedited shipping. Monday, she would drive to Kalispell and try to buy what she hadn't found online. Monday evening, they would meet again and decide how to find or make whatever items they still needed.

Amy grabbed the sweater she'd brought from

the house and stuck her arms in the sleeves for warmth against the nighttime chill. "We should probably talk about the cost of all this."

"It's not a problem. I'll pay you back for anything you have to buy."

"Derek, come on. It's a lot more than the decorations and games. I totally intend to pay for that stuff myself. But there's still food and drinks. And what about the venue and the music?"

"It's covered," he said.

"Covered?" She couldn't help scoffing. "All of it?"

He shrugged. "I told you that Nate Crawford offered the Manor. And he offered it at a deep discount, believe me. Just about everyone in town will be there and that's good PR for the Manor. There'll be plenty of finger food. As for alcohol, Hudson is footing the bill for the champagne and soft drinks." Hudson Jones, a very wealthy man, was Bella Stockton's husband. "I promise I'm good for whatever the final bill amounts to." And then he laughed. "Don't look so worried. I'm not the same broke-ass cowboy you used to know."

"I'm not worried. Really."

"Oh, yeah, you are. But you don't need to be. I'm doing all right. You remember Collin Traub?"

"Of course." Collin had been in their graduating class. "Eva told me that Collin married Willa Christensen." Willa was younger. She'd graduated a few years after them. "Eva also mentioned that Collin's the mayor now. But what has Collin Traub got to do with how we plan to split up the cost of the bachelor party?"

"Collin's uncle Casper had a saddle-making business, which Collin inherited when Casper passed on. I hooked up with Collin a while back. Besides working the family ranch, I make saddles and a variety of fine leather goods. I've kind of built a name for myself—and earned some good money, too."

Leatherwork. He'd always had a talent for that. He used to make pretty beaded leather jewelry for her. And for her eighteenth birthday, he'd made her a leather vest and a fringed skirt. She'd loved them and worn them proudly. Still had them, too, tucked in the back of her closet.

Because she never could quite bear to get rid of them.

"We have a shop on Sawmill Street, at North Broomtail Road," he said.

"CT Saddles, right?"

"That's it."

"I drove by it the other day. And I'm glad

that you're doing so well—but, Derek, I want to pitch in, too. I *am* the maid of honor, after all, and I should pay half."

He looked at her for a long time. She felt the sudden presence of the past—*their* past—rising up in the darkness between them.

What had he said?

I'm not the same broke-ass cowboy you used to know.

It wasn't that he came from a poor family. The Daltons had been ranching in the Rust Creek Falls Valley for generations and his dad was a leader in the community, a lawyer with an office in town. Still, back in high school, Derek hadn't had much, not in terms of cash in hand. When they ran away to Kalispell, he'd bought her a simulated diamond ring for forty dollars at Walmart.

She'd thrown it at him the day he told her to get her stuff and go with her dad. Where was that ring now? What had he done with it?

Not that she'd ever ask.

"Okay then," the grown-up Derek said. "We'll go fifty-fifty on the final bill."

"Perfect. Thank you. Now, let me see…" She woke her phone, punched up the party file again and brought up the dual lists of what had to be bought and what would need to be made or otherwise assembled.

"How we doin'?" he asked.

She gave him a nod. "Really well, actually."

"You feel like we're getting somewhere with this party, then?"

"I do. And I think we're pretty much set for now."

Their non-date was almost over.

And somehow, they'd managed to steer clear of the past—mostly, anyway.

All good, she told herself. It was the past, after all, over and done, and they didn't need to go there.

But then he stretched out on his back, laced his hands beneath his head and stared up at the wide indigo sky. "Lots of stars out tonight, Miss Wainwright."

Miss Wainwright.

Their private joke. He'd called her that in their first tutoring session and it had stuck.

"Yes, Miss Wainwright," he would tease her.

"Whatever you say, Miss Wainwright."

"Miss Wainwright, you're the boss."

He looked pretty comfortable, lying there. Not like he planned to get up and leave anytime soon.

Maybe the evening wasn't over, after all.

Chapter 3

Feeling light as air suddenly, and dangerously playful, Amy took his hat off the blanket and put it on. It was too big, and slipped down over her eyes.

Laughing, she tipped her head back. "Yeah. Lots of stars. A beautiful night."

"You forgive me, for not calling?"

"Yeah." She said it softly. "Thank you for the picnic. I...feel better about everything."

He was watching her so steadily. "You're as pretty as you ever were, Miss Wainwright—hell, you're prettier."

She felt the blush as it swept up her neck and over her cheeks. But what with the darkness, she doubted he could see it. She opened her mouth to say something teasing and light. But the memories were pressing in again and somehow, a raw truth slipped out. "I've had a crush on you since I was thirteen."

It was an old confession, one she'd made to him long ago, at a party on New Year's Eve, the night he told her for the first time that she was everything he'd ever wanted.

Her heart had ached with sheer happiness that night. How impossibly young she'd been, young and absolutely certain that nothing could ever tear them apart.

He reached up, took his hat off her head and set it on his chest. "You never would look at me. Not when you were thirteen or fourteen or fifteen…"

"I had no clue you might be looking at me. Not until that first tutoring session."

He grunted. "You were seventeen. And you still wouldn't look at me, even then."

"So, shoot me. I was shy. But it didn't take that long once we were stuck in a room together. By the end of that first session, I *was* looking at you, and right in the eye, too. I started getting the feeling then that just maybe you liked me—but then, I told myself, you liked all the girls."

"Uh-uh." His eyes shone almost black in the moonlight, holding hers. "I only wanted *you*."

"You asked me out." She couldn't help grinning. "I turned you down."

"But I persisted," he said.

"Oh, yes, you did." By Christmas of that year, she totally got that the hottest guy in school was crazy about her. Then at New Year's, he'd said he wasn't looking at any other girl. And he proved it, too. He was all about her, about Amy. And it felt so good to be wanted by a guy at last—not to mention by the sexiest, most charming guy in the whole school.

"My dad taught me that," he said.

"Taught you what?"

"To persist. 'Son,' he used to say, 'above all, if you want something, *persist*.' He always said *persist* with emphasis, you know?"

Amy remembered Charles Dalton as a kind, intelligent man.

"I always liked your dad." She brushed his shoulder, realized that touching him was maybe a bridge too far, and quickly withdrew her hand. "Um, your mom, too."

He stared up at the sky for a string of too-quiet seconds before asking, "How are *your* parents?"

"They're well. My dad retired two years ago.

They moved to San Diego. They seem to like it there. My mom's in a bunch of clubs—book clubs, bridge clubs. He plays a lot of golf."

"Well, good," Derek said. He was watching her again, his eyes so deep, she wanted to fall in and never come out.

There had been no love lost between Derek and her mom and dad. They'd checked and found out that he was not a great student and would likely never even go to college. Derek only wanted to live on his family's ranch and work all day running cattle. He wasn't what her parents had in mind for her, their precious only daughter.

Her dad and mom had made it very clear that they wanted her to stop seeing "that Dalton boy." Amy defied them. She stood right up to them and said she would see him anyway, that he was the best thing that had ever happened to her.

They must have realized she meant what she'd said, because they'd backed off.

And after that, she and Derek spent every spare moment together. That New Year's Eve, when he'd said he loved her, she'd believed him and declared her love right back. He promised there would never be anyone but her. Amy wanted him so much and he wanted her and, well, it was young love.

She couldn't wait to have it all—all the kisses, the caresses, the soft, secret sighs. Making love was bound to happen.

And it did. In the early spring.

It was scary, that first time. Scary and a little awkward. But, oh so beautiful.

Already set to go to the University of Colorado on a full scholarship in the fall, Amy turned eighteen in May. In early June, she and Derek both graduated from Rust Creek Falls High.

"Remember graduation?" she asked, lost in the past now.

He made a low noise in the affirmative. "I remember your speech as valedictorian. 'We don't have to be perfect. We just have to do the best that we can every day, as we go forward into a future full of promise and the challenge of—'"

"Please." She cut him off with a groan. "No more. There is no way I was ever that young."

"Yeah, you were." He reached up, brushed a rough-tender finger along her cheek, leaving a sweet trail of lingering sensation in his wake. "So was I. We were *that* young. And you were all set, with a big future ahead of you. I never wanted to hold you back."

"I know that."

"We were *too* young."

She bit her lip, knowing he was right. She'd wanted to go to CU, wanted a good job that challenged her, and she'd doubted she would find that job in their tiny Montana town. At the same time, she hadn't known how she would live without the boy she loved.

He said, "Think about it this way. It all ended up according to plan."

"Right. Just with that big, painful detour stuck in the middle of it."

Because by the end of June, her period was late. She'd waited a week and it didn't come. She went to Derek. He drove her to Kalispell to buy a test and they rented a cheap room where she took that test.

She shivered a little and wrapped her sweater closer around her. "I was so scared when the test came out positive. And you took a knee right there in that motel room."

"I wanted to marry you, Amy. I really did."

She stared down at him, saw the moon reflected in his eyes. "I know. And I loved you. So much."

"It was the Fourth of July. There were fireworks going off all night long, remember?"

Oh, yes, she did. "I remember."

The next day, the fifth of July, they went to the courthouse and said *I do*, just the two of them, two scared kids with a baby on the way.

And for their honeymoon, they returned to the cheap room with its lumpy bed. At night, she could hear the trucks whizzing by on the highway.

"You were sorry, though, weren't you?" he asked. "Sorry from the first."

"It was only that I—"

"Don't lie," he said gently. "Let's just tell each other the truth now, okay, and be done with it?"

"Yeah. All right." She admitted, "I, well, I had serious second thoughts."

"I knew it." At least he didn't sound angry.

But why should he? It was so long ago. And this wasn't any big confession. This was making peace. With the past.

With each other.

This was putting it behind them, once and for all.

She said, "I just had trouble coping, you know? With my whole life turned around and a baby on the way." She really had loved him. But it had all just seemed so overwhelming.

The next day and the day after that, he drove back to the Circle D to work. She stayed in Kalispell. She had a cell phone, though reception in the area was hit and miss back then. Her parents kept calling her. She let the calls go to voice mail for three days and then she finally answered and told them she had married Derek. Her dad demanded to know where she was. She hung up on him.

"And then, the night of the fourth day," she said in a raggedy whisper, "my period came."

Had she lost the baby? Or had she never been pregnant in the first place? Who knew?

"That hurt," he said. "I mean, the baby had turned everything upside down. But suddenly, there was no baby and somehow, that was even worse."

She agreed with a slow nod.

The next day—the fifth and final day—to cheer her up, he'd taken her to visit the Armstrongs while he went to work at the ranch.

Nobody knew that she'd married him—except the two of them and her parents. She'd made him promise not to tell his family until she was ready. When his mom and dad asked questions about where he got off to every night, he just said he was fine and for them not to worry. His parents had let it go at that. After all, he was nineteen, old enough to stay out all night if he wanted to. And besides, their ill-fated elopement didn't last long. Before Rita and Charles Dalton got around to insisting that Derek tell them what was going on, it was over.

That day, the fifth day, when he dropped her off at the Armstrongs', she had longed to confide in her friends—maybe not Eva, who was only thirteen at the time. But Delphine and Calla, definitely. They were like sisters to her.

She just couldn't do it, though, couldn't tell them what she was going through. They knew she was really upset about something and they hugged her and fussed over her. They told her that, whatever it was, it would be all right, that they would always be there for her, no matter what.

She asked Derek, "Did I tell you that Delphine quizzed me about you that day? She wanted to know if something had gone wrong between the two of us." Everyone knew she'd been dating Derek, and the Armstrongs had seen him drop her off that morning.

"No, you never told me that. You hardly said a word on the drive back to the motel in Kalispell."

"I was all turned around inside, so sad about losing the baby, wondering how it was all going to work out."

"I remember." His voice was flat. Bleak.

And then he asked, "What did you say to her that day—to Delphine?"

"I just shook my head and promised that I was fine and so were you."

"But she guessed you were lying."

"Yeah. I'll bet they all three did."

"Even Eva? She was so young."

"But she's always been sensitive to what other people are going through."

"That day," he said, staring up at the dark sky, "was the end of it…"

The end of us, she thought. "After that day, I never saw you again until last Monday, right here at the farm."

"Thirteen years," he said, his voice so heavy. With regret? With sadness or maybe bitterness? She couldn't have said and she didn't quite have the nerve to ask him what exactly he was feeling right now.

Instead, she got on with it. "I have no idea how my dad knew to find us at that motel. I never told him where I was. I assumed he'd somehow followed us from the Armstrongs' house. I asked Eva's mom later, before I left for Boulder, if she had called my dad and told him I was there that day. She swore she hadn't." Derek said nothing. He stared at the sky. Somewhere nearby, a lone owl hooted. A shiver ran through her. She peered down at him more closely. "What?"

He shifted his gaze to meet hers. "I didn't say anything."

"I thought maybe you were about to."

"Uh-uh."

She drew in a slow breath. "Well, however he did it, my father figured it out."

Derek stared up into her night-shadowed eyes. Her skin was so smooth, silvered in moonlight.

He knew how her father had found them. But he wasn't going to tell her. What good would that do? Jack Wainwright wasn't a bad man. He'd just wanted the best for his only child and he'd followed them from the Armstrongs', followed them to Kalispell and that cheap motel.

At the sight of her dad emerging from his fancy pickup, looking grim and exhausted, Amy had started to cry.

Derek had hated himself then, for jumping the gun and begging her to marry him, for putting her in this position, for messing everything up.

He didn't know what to do next. Amy had gotten pregnant—or maybe not. She'd lost the baby—or maybe not. Because how can you lose something that never was?

He'd known she was miserable that day, known she regretted running away with him. She'd had such big plans for herself and there she was, a not-pregnant married woman who wasn't going to go to college, after all.

As he'd watched the tears tracking down her cheeks that July afternoon, Derek felt his heart shatter into a million pieces. He and Jack Wainwright agreed on one thing, at least: that run-down motel wasn't good enough for Amy.

And what did Derek think he was going to do next? Move his bride into the bunkhouse with him at the Circle D? Or into the main house where his parents lived? Damn, but the truth he faced then was the hardest one of all.

He'd yet to get a real start in life and would need to depend on his family to help support her. And she? Amy deserved the best. With the baby gone, well, why shouldn't she have the future she'd always planned on? His pride had felt frayed raw at all he couldn't give her.

Now, in the low light of the lantern, she softly accused, "When my dad asked me to come home with him, you said I should go."

He wasn't about to try to make her see how he'd really felt. Better to just confirm what she already knew. "That's right. It's what I said."

"I wondered then if you would be relieved

to get rid of me..." She'd had her dad wait outside and she led Derek into their little room. "I did tell you that I loved you."

He could reassure her on that point, at least. "I know you did. I'll never forget that you did."

"I said I did want my education, but couldn't we find a way to be husband and wife, *and* for me to go to CU?"

"Listen. All I felt then was that I was holding you back. I looked in those big eyes of yours and I saw that you needed to be free to live your bright future without being tied down to a guy who couldn't even support you."

"But I *wanted* to be with you."

"Don't." He sat up. "You wanted the future you deserved. There's nothing wrong with that."

She shook her head at him. "Oh, Derek—"

"It wasn't going to work."

"But if we—"

"No. Uh-uh. We needed to let go."

She accused, "That day, you said it was all a big mistake."

"And it was, wasn't it? I mean, there was no baby, or the baby was lost. Whichever it was, we'd just run off and gotten married without thinking things over."

"You said you didn't really want to be married, anyway."

"Yeah, Amy. I did. That's what I said." It was a lie, but it was way too late to tell her that now.

She sat up straighter and tossed her ponytail, defiant, more than a little bit angry. "So, I agreed with you. I said we'd made a mistake and you were right, we just needed to put it behind us. That was when you said I should get my stuff and go with my dad. I threw my ring at you." Her slim shoulders drooped. "I just want you to know I've always regretted doing that. I did love that ring. And you. Oh, Derek, I loved you so much. I'm so sorry that I—"

"Stop." He couldn't stand how he'd hurt her, how they'd hurt each other. "It's okay." He knew he shouldn't, but he reached out anyway. He curled a hand around the back of her neck and drew her close.

"Derek." She sagged against him, wrapped her soft arms around him. He breathed in the scent of her, so sweet, so right.

"I'm sorry, too," he whispered. "About all of it." He stroked the silky hair pulled tight at her temple. There were things he shouldn't say. But he had to let at least a little of the truth shine through. "You were everything to me."

"Oh, Derek. And *you* were, to me."

He took her face between his hands. "We can't go back and do it over. And even if we could, who's to say how it might have turned out? We both had a lot of growing up to do."

Her gaze searched his. "We should have tried. We might have made it."

He gave her ponytail a teasing little tug. "We're never going to know what might have happened."

She pressed her lips together, sniffled just a little—and smiled. "Yeah. You're right. I know you are. And I'm glad. That we talked about it. I mean, there is no blame here. Things turned out for the best, don't you think?"

What could he say to that, except, "Absolutely."

"And we're over it."

He never would be, not really. But what good would it do either of them to admit that now? "Yeah, we are."

The moment stretched out. She gazed up at him, all soft and trusting. How could he stop himself?

He didn't *want* to stop himself.

He lowered his mouth just enough to brush hers.

Heaven. Kissing Amy was heaven.

Not in years and years had he dared to imagine that someday he would kiss her again.

With a sweet, hungry cry, she surged up onto her knees and slid her arms more firmly around him. She tasted so good, opening to him. Inviting him inside.

He dipped his tongue into all that sweetness and she moaned against his mouth.

More. The word thrummed through his blood. He wanted more of her. He felt sweet desire and a longing so deep—for all that they'd had. All that was lost.

All that he should have sense enough to realize would never be again.

They'd been kids, innocent. Trusting.

Now they were all grown-up. She had her life in Boulder and she would go back to it as soon as Eva married Luke.

The past was just that: done. Over. Gone.

And it needed to stay gone.

With way more regret than he should have allowed himself, he lifted his mouth from hers.

Her eyes slowly opened. She gazed up at him, unspeaking, her expression kind of dreamy. He could have sat there just looking at her forever.

But really, he'd been cradling her beautiful face for much too long. He let his hands drop away.

She sank back on her folded knees, coming to rest on her heels. "Well. That was…unexpected."

"Just a kiss," he said, and way too gruffly.

Slowly, she nodded. "Yeah. Just a kiss."

He saw questions in her eyes. "What? Go ahead and ask."

"You sure?"

"How can I answer until you ask me the question?"

"It's just that I always wondered. Do you still have my ring?"

He shrugged, a lying shrug. But it was better that way. "What can I tell you? I don't remember what I did with it."

"Oh, God." With a soft groan, she covered her face with her palms. And then she slanted him an embarrassed glance. "I am hopeless. Sorry."

"Nothing to be sorry about." For another long stretch of seconds, they just looked at each other. He broke the silence. "It's after eleven. We should probably call it a night."

"Yeah."

They gathered up the remains of their picnic, piled it all in the basket and folded up the blanket. She stuck her big phone in a pocket of her jeans and carried the lantern, lighting their way as they returned to the house and his waiting truck. When they got there, he put the blanket and basket in on the passenger side. She handed him the lantern. He switched it off and set it in the truck, too.

Finally, he shut the door and turned to her.

Luke and Eva had apparently come home and they'd left the porch light on. Amy and Derek stood close together, just beyond the golden circle of light.

"It's meant a lot to me," she said, her eyes so steady, holding his, "the things we said tonight."

"To me, too."

"I feel better about everything. Better about us."

"So do I."

She sank her pretty teeth into her lower lip, glanced away and then back. "I just want you to know that I'm not trying to get anything started."

"I get it, Amy. I completely understand."

"It could never go anywhere."

He wanted only to reach for her again, to claim those soft lips one more time. "You're right," he said, and kept his hands to himself. "But about Monday…"

"Yeah?" Did she sound a little breathless?

Pleasure flowed through him. She might talk about how what they'd had was long over, how they'd get no second chances. But the look in her eyes said otherwise. He tried not to smile. "I'll be at the saddlery all day."

She drew a sharp little breath that sounded a lot like anticipation. "I could meet you there when I get back from shopping in Kalispell. Say at five? You could give me a tour, show me some of your work."

"Five is good. And after the tour, we'll go on out to Maverick Manor for that burger I promised you. You can see the venue, the main meeting room we'll be using and the smaller adjoining room where I thought we would set up the casino."

"Another non-date, right?" she teased, the left corner of her too-damn-kissable mouth hitching up just a fraction, a cute dimple tucking itself into her soft cheek.

"Yep. 'Cause you and me, we aren't getting anything started."

"Oh, no, we are not."

"We're firmly in the friend zone."

"Friends," she repeated. "I'm all for that."

He went around to the driver's side and climbed in. She followed, standing back a little as he turned the engine over. He leaned out the window to tip his hat at her. "'Night, Miss Wainwright."

Her smile bloomed full out. "You are so bad, Derek Dalton."

He gave her a wave and got the hell out of

there before he threw all his good intentions out the window, jumped from the truck and showed her just how bad he could be.

Sunday morning, Eva made waffles. When Amy came downstairs, Luke and Bailey were already at the table, chowing down on the delicious food—which, Amy eagerly observed, included fresh fruit and whipped cream and pure maple syrup.

Bailey lived in one of Sunshine Farm's seven cabins, which Rob Stockton, the family patriarch, had built years ago in hopes that his children might stay to raise their own kids on the family homestead. Though Bailey liked his privacy, he often came to the main house to eat. Nobody with a pulse could resist Eva's cooking. Not even a gruff, independent man like Bailey Stockton.

Eva, at the waffle iron, glanced over her shoulder when Amy entered the kitchen. "Pour yourself some coffee," she commanded with a radiant smile, secure in her role as queen of the kitchen. "And have a seat. Your breakfast is almost ready."

Amy savored the excellent coffee and sighed in delight when Eva slid a golden, perfect waffle in front of her. "Eva, you are a goddess of the culinary arts and I love you with all of my heart." Laughing, Eva pulled out the chair next to her and sat down. Amy frowned at her. "Where's yours?"

"I already ate. What's up for you today?"

"Mostly, I'll be upstairs working—and ordering a bunch of stuff online for the bachelor party."

Eva braced her elbow on the table, propped her chin on her hand and remarked with overplayed innocence, "We saw Derek's truck out in front when we got home last night."

Amy ate an amazing bite of waffle, fresh peaches and whipped cream, after which she gave her friend a look of great patience. "We took a meeting in a nice, grassy spot not that far from the barn. It was a very productive meeting, so productive that I actually think we've got this party under control."

Lazily, Eva drew a heart on the table with her index finger. "It was a very long meeting." She stretched out the word *long* until it had about ten syllables in it. "I didn't hear that truck of his leave until after eleven."

"Big party. Lots of planning to do."

Eva glanced across at the men.

Luke met his fiancée's eyes and stood as though on cue. "Come on, Bailey, let's get after it."

Bailey gulped down a last sip of coffee and rose, too. They carried their plates to the sink and went out the back door.

Eva got up, poured herself some coffee and topped off Amy's cup. Then she sat back down again. "I know you really loved him. And he really loved you. And I have to say, the chemistry between you two? Still off the charts."

"Eva, don't exaggerate."

"I'm not. I saw the way you looked at each other Friday night at the Ace in the Hole. And when you were dancing with him?" She made a big show of fanning herself. "It's like you were the only two people in the place."

Amy licked a dab of whipped cream from her upper lip, sipped more coffee—and reminded herself that Eva didn't need to know all the secrets that were better left safely in the past. "You're imagining things."

"Oh, please. I don't think so."

"Derek and I are friends, that's all. Casual friends."

Eva leaned close and spoke softly. "All I'm saying is, maybe give it a chance, you know? Anything might happen. But you have to be open. You have to be ready to let love in."

"I don't think so."

Eva shook a finger at her. "Wrong attitude."

"No. We agreed we weren't going to get anything started."

"We?"

"Eva, please. You know who. Derek and I."

"When, last night?"

"That's right."

"Oh, Amy." Eva fluttered her eyelashes. "You and I both know an agreement like that is just made to be broken."

Chapter 4

After spending much of Sunday ordering party supplies, Amy headed for Kalispell on Monday morning. By four thirty, she'd been to six different stores that sold party supplies, equipment and games—four in Kalispell and two in nearby Columbia Falls. The back of her Audi Q5 was piled high with shopping bags.

She headed for Rust Creek Falls to meet Derek, feeling really good about all she'd accomplished since their meeting by lantern-light Saturday night.

True, the closer she got to seeing him again, the more anxious she felt—an anticipatory sort of anxiousness, complete with flutters in her tummy and a suddenly racing heart. By the time she parked in a space in front of the tin-roofed building with the long wooden porch and the CT Saddles sign across the front, she was a bundle of nerves, but in a giddy kind of way.

And then she saw Derek, in jeans, brown boots and a black T-shirt, looking like every red-blooded girl's fantasy cowboy, waiting on the porch beneath the sign. He came down the steps and pulled her door open for her.

"Nice car." He offered his hand.

She took it and a hot little thrill shivered up her arm. *Friends*, she reminded herself resolutely. *We are friends.* "Thank you." She stepped out.

He shut the door and peeked in the back window. "Looks like you raided every party store in the state of Montana."

"Stick with me." She smoothed her skinny jeans, a nervous gesture and totally unnecessary. Skinny jeans were much too snug to wrinkle. "I know how to shop."

He laughed, the sound deep and free. Easy.

She thought about what Eva had said, that she should be open, give love a chance—okay, maybe not love. That was in the past.

But she did definitely feel the zing of attraction every time she saw him. Being open to whatever might happen, well, that couldn't be wrong, could it?

He leaned close and the flutters in her tummy intensified. "You smell like wildflowers. And you've got a secret kind of smile on your face. What's going on in that big brain of yours, anyway?"

She nudged him with a playful elbow. "I'm all about the party plans. You should see the decorations I got for the casino. Everything in red, white and black. Giant dice stacked at the door. Straw cowboy hats to go with the whole Western theme."

"That secret smile is about party plans?"

"Well, yeah, and seeing what goes on at CT Saddles—oh, and that burger you promised me. I need that soon. All the shopping has given me an appetite."

Her hair was loose. He guided a stray curl back over her shoulder, his finger lightly brushing the side of her neck, stirring up lovely, shivery sensations.

Just friends, she told herself yet again, and tried to believe it.

His finger skated down her arm, causing her nerve endings to spark and flare as it went. He caught her hand.

It felt so right, his touch.

Warm and rough and protective and tender.

And really, she needed *not* to get carried away.

"Come on inside," he said, and pulled her toward the steps.

He showed her his worktables—a butcher block–topped one for laying out patterns and cutting leather, with a huge array of tools on a long, moveable rack overhead. And another for tooling, with a solid slate top mounted on two-by-fours, so the surface had no give in it when he hit the leather to punch in his designs. His hole punches, mauls, chisels and stamps were waiting in a series of racks all around, easy to reach as he worked.

He introduced her to a dark-haired boy in his teens. "This is Ned Faraday. He's working with us for the summer."

Ned set aside the broom he'd been sweeping up scraps with and shook her hand. "Nice to meet you," he said shyly.

"You planning on being a saddle-maker?" she asked him.

"Yes, I am. I like the work…and it keeps me out of trouble." He kind of mumbled that last.

He seemed like a great kid. She couldn't resist asking, "You get in trouble a lot, Ned?"

"Used to," he replied, and got to work with the broom again.

Derek clapped him on the shoulder. "It's after five. You can go ahead and take off now."

"Monday, same as usual?" Ned asked eagerly. Apparently, he loved his job.

"Yeah. See you at nine." As he spoke to Ned, Derek put a hand to the small of Amy's back, a sweetly proprietary gesture that made her feel catered to, cared for. Really, she needed to watch herself or she'd be head-over-heels for the guy all over again. He leaned close. His warm breath kissed her ear. "Let me show you a couple of my projects." He guided her across the room to the rows of saddletrees.

She was vaguely aware of the door closing as Ned left, but mostly she was blown away by the saddle in front of her. "Wow." She reached out and touched the supple, intricately tooled fender. "This is from *Alarica*, right?" She named the wildly popular video game in which robots had taken over the world and gone to war with each other.

"You guessed it."

"Wow," she said again for lack of a word good enough.

"A long way from a leather vest and a fringed skirt, huh?" He slanted her one his almost-smiles.

"I loved that vest and skirt," she informed him and tried to decide whether to admit she still had them, that she never could bear to let them go. But no. To confess that seemed unbearably intimate, somehow. And they were not getting intimate. They were keeping it friendly, easy and light. "This is perfection, Derek." She stroked the barrel of a futuristic weapon, ran her finger down the perfectly pin-hinged hip of the robot temptress, Dellarue, who seduced her challengers before killing them.

"Collin does the classic Western stuff," he explained. "I'm getting known for the weird projects and I like it that way. I did a whole series of saddles for an El Baharian sheikh, scenes from famous battles in the history of El Bahar. This one, though, was commissioned by Lincoln Copes, the creator of *Alarica*. He's got a ranch in Idaho not far from Sundance where he breeds Arabians."

He also showed her saddlebags tooled with exotic twining flowers—orchids, anthuriums, jasmine, hibiscus—and another saddle decorated with stars and moons.

"They're all so gorgeous."

He took her arm and turned her around to face him. "You sound impressed."

"I am. All this is, well, I think I may be running out of adjectives. I knew you had talent for working with leather. I just didn't realize how far you would take it."

"All the way." He touched her hair again, wrapping a curl of it around his finger. The moment felt just next-door to the intimacy they weren't supposed to be sharing and she enjoyed it way too much.

Taking his sweet time over it, he unwrapped that curl and let his hand drop away, after which they shared a long, lovely moment where all they did was stare at each other and grin.

"Tell me about Ned," she suggested after what felt like forever. "What did he mean that working here keeps him out of trouble?"

"His mom died a few years ago."

"That's hard."

"Yeah. He was an only kid, close to his mom. And he didn't get along that well with his dad. He started acting out."

"After she died, you mean?"

"Right."

"How old is he?"

"Sixteen now. Last year, when he was fifteen, he kind of lost it. Broke into his dad's liquor cabinet and got drunk, wandered over to Crawford's General Store—at night, when the store was closed—and threw rocks in the windows."

"Oh, no."

"Oh, yeah." He backed up a little and sat on an empty saddle stand. Shaking his head, he went on, "Then he came here, broke another window and climbed in it. Didn't do much damage, really, other than the busted window. But he did trigger the alarm. After it rang for a minute or two, he realized he would probably get caught if he tried to hide out in the saddlery, so he jumped back out the window and took off down North Broomtail Road—right past the sheriff's office. Gage Christensen, who's the sheriff now, caught him and locked him up in the jail to put the fear of the law in him."

"Poor kid."

"Yeah. Once he sobered up a little, Ned was scared to death he was going straight to the state pen. Kind of woke up Ned's dad, too. He agreed to get family counseling with Ned. We—me and Collin and the Crawfords—offered Ned the chance to work part-time at the general store and here at the saddlery to pay for the damage he'd done. Long story short,

Ned and his dad are getting along better after counseling and Ned found out he likes making things from leather. The kid's got talent for it, too. Once he worked off his debt, he asked if maybe we would keep him on. He works a few hours on the weekends during the school year and twenty hours a week now that it's summer vacation."

"A happy ending, then."

"You could say that." He watched her so closely, his hot gaze tracking from her mouth to her eyes and back again. It sent a happy little thrill rushing through her, the way he looked at her, even if happy little thrills weren't the kind of thing she should be letting him inspire in her.

She gave herself a mental shake. "I love it when bad stuff turns good—and it's so great, what you and Collin and the Crawfords did, giving Ned a way to turn things around for himself."

He shrugged off her praise. "Hey, it's Rust Creek Falls. Everything always ends happily here."

"So they say." Tenderness welled in her. Yeah, he had that sexy edge of the hot guy all the girls sighed over. But he was also a *good* guy, always had been. "And you never could take a compliment." When he made a scoffing sound, she insisted, "I mean it, Derek. You did reach out and help Ned when he needed it. Don't brush me off when I say I admire what you did."

He stood and stepped closer. "All right, then." He smelled so good, of leather and man. Another sweet, endless glance passed between them. "Thank you."

"That's better."

He took her hand. His touch felt so right, stirring old memories, making her wish he might never let go. "Now how 'bout that fancy burger?"

"Sounds great." And much less dangerous than being here alone with him where who knew what kind of mischief she might be tempted to get up to. "I'll follow you."

He rubbed his thumb across the back of her hand. Such a simple caress, yet it stirred her. Too much. "You might as well just ride with me."

Was she tempted? Oh, yes. But somehow, she managed to shake her head. "Then you'd just have to bring me all the way back here to get my car."

"I wouldn't mind. Not one bit." He dipped his dark head a fraction closer, that unruly hair of his flopping on his forehead, just begging her to reach up and smooth it back.

"Derek?" Her voice sounded downright husky.

"Hmm?"

"I'm taking my own car."

Now he was the one shaking his head. "Have it your way."

"I believe I will." She couldn't stifle a slow grin.

"You're acting kind of naughty, Miss Wainwright."

She let her grin get even wider. "Maybe. A little." It was only flirting, after all. And it felt wonderful.

Still holding her hand, he turned for the door.

At Maverick Manor, they parked side by side in the lot by the main entrance.

"Wait a minute," she said, when he stepped up and opened her car door for her. "Isn't this…?"

"Bledsoe's Folly?" He took her hand and she let him. "The one and only." The imposing log home had been built way back in the '80s by an eccentric multimillionaire who later lost it all when the market crashed. "Bledsoe's original log mansion is the center of Maverick Manor."

"It looks great. And even bigger."

"They added on, of course, but kept the log cabin–style throughout."

Inside, he gave her a quick tour—from the giant central lobby with its impressive mural honoring the founding families of Rust Creek Falls to the meeting rooms they would be using for the party. They went outside and strolled the grounds, lush and green in high summer, and then checked out the dining room. Finally, they took seats in the bar and enjoyed giant, juicy burgers with hot, crispy fries. She got out her phone and they went over the few things she'd yet to find for the party.

"Text the list to me," he said. "I'll see how many I can get and then, if we have to, we'll figure out something else to do for the rest."

"You're sure? Because I don't mind—"

He put his hand over hers, tucking his thumb all cozy in the cove of her palm. Little flares of pleasure spiked along her nerve endings. "I've got this. Give me tomorrow to work on it. I'll come by Sunshine Farm tomorrow after dinner. Say, seven?"

"Seven works." She picked up the check. He tried to snatch it from her. "Uh-uh. You brought me a picnic. I'm good for the burgers."

He walked her out to her car. It was almost

nine by then, dusk painting the sky in layers of vivid color.

He asked her about her job. "Luke said you track down the bad guys online."

"More or less." She launched into an explanation of the growing prevalence of digital fraud and how her work entailed staying one step ahead of embezzlers, hackers and other internet criminals. "I work mostly at home."

"Doesn't that get lonely?"

"Not really. I make my own hours. Sometimes they're very long hours when the situation is urgent and I need to produce a report in a short time frame. On the other hand, nobody complains if I'm not at my desk nine to five. It's a great job that holds my interest. Never boring, you know?"

"Kind of like fixing fences," he joked.

But she didn't laugh. "Well, you need to keep those cattle where you put them and I need to keep the money in the hands of the people it actually belongs to, so yeah. Kind of like fixing fences."

She could have stood there in that parking lot with him, talking about nothing in particular, all night long.

But when she reluctantly turned to open her

door, he reached around and did it for her. She got in. He waved as she drove away.

He knocked on the farmhouse door at seven sharp the next night. She ushered him and he said hi to Eva and Luke.

Eva asked, "Did you eat?" When he said he had, she offered, "How about a fat slice of loganberry pie, then?"

"Eva." He gave her his killer grin. "If you baked it, I'm in."

Derek and Luke sat at the table, eating pie and drinking coffee, discussing alfalfa crop yields and beef prices as Amy helped Eva load the dishwasher with the dinner dishes and wipe down the counters.

It was nice, Amy thought. Homey. The four of them in the kitchen, the good smells of coffee and the banana bread Eva had baking in the oven, the deep, easy sounds of the men's voices as they talked about everyday things.

Like a fantasy, really. A faint, sweet echo of the life she'd once imagined for herself. This was how it would have been if she and Derek had stayed together and she'd become a ranch wife—while somehow also managing to get her degree and a great job that challenged her.

"What?" asked Eva softly.

Amy realized she was just standing at the counter, staring off into space with a dish towel in one hand and the cut crystal relish plate in the other. "Um, nothing. Not a thing."

Eva's bright blue eyes actually seemed to twinkle. "Yeah, right."

Amy insisted, "Really. Nothing. I was thinking about nothing."

Eva laughed, but said no more.

A few minutes later, out on the porch again, Derek and Amy went over the dwindling list of party supplies they still needed and agreed on substitutes for what they hadn't found. She insisted that he let her look for those.

Then they climbed in his pickup and drove to the yellow barn, where they added the things he'd rounded up that day to the growing pile of goodies Luke had let them store in the tack room.

By the time they finished that small chore it was half past eight—and she just didn't want him to go.

She perched on a hay bale and willed him to sit down next to her. "We should talk about setup, don't you think? I know it's eleven days until the party, but it can't hurt to get everything planned out in advance."

"Fair enough." He hooked his hat on a tack

hanger and dropped to her side, right where she wanted him.

Yes, she was being thoroughly bad, to keep urging him closer when she should let him go. But somehow, she couldn't help herself. She never could resist being bad when it came to him. Some things, apparently, never changed.

She'd been the shiest girl at Rust Creek Falls High—until she and Derek had gotten together. After that New Year's Eve when they'd declared their young love to each other, she'd become totally shameless in her need to be near him as often as possible.

"I talked to the manager over at the Manor," he said. "We can get in there to start setting up at 6:00 a.m."

"And the party starts at seven that night…" She tipped her head to the side as though considering what he'd just told her. In reality, her senses were on overload. He was so close, his warm, hard thigh touching hers. "It should be totally doable," she said, biting her lower lip, pretending to be deep in thought.

"Yeah," he replied, drawing out the word, his head turned her way, his gaze on her mouth. "Doable."

It was delicious, this shivery excitement spreading all through her. "Delphine and Calla and their families are driving in the day before, on Friday." Her own voice surprised her, sounding so calm and unaffected. "They'll pitch in, along with their husbands and kids." Eva's sisters, along with Luke's sisters, Bella and Dana, Jamie's wife, Fallon, and Danny's wife, Annie, were all to be bridesmaids. "Dana will be coming Friday, as well." Last born of the seven Stockton siblings, Dana lived in Oregon. She would be staying with Bella and Hudson until after the wedding.

"And you know we'll get Bailey, Danny and Jamie to help," he added. Luke's brothers were the other groomsmen. "Plus, whoever else we can get to volunteer."

"It'll work. Thirteen hours or so should be plenty of time to set it all up."

"Okay, then." He rose.

No! cried the romantic fool within her. *Not yet. Don't go yet.*

But he was already standing above her. "Unless you need me for anything in the meantime," he said, "we're all set until 6:00 a.m. a week from Saturday. If I don't hear from you before then, I'll call you and touch base next Tuesday, just to be sure we're up to speed."

She had the insane urge to grab his hand and yank him back down onto the hay bale with her. Really, this was so weak and wrong of her. They'd agreed that the past was the past and they'd grown beyond it. They were friends by necessity until Eva and Luke walked down the aisle.

"When did you and Luke get to be friends?" The question just burst out of her, sounding slightly squeaky with a weird, desperate edge. And she was desperate. Because she wanted to keep him there and all her good sense had flown out the tack room door.

He didn't answer right away, just gazed down at her with a musing expression. Really, it wasn't fair in the least. He had those beautiful green eyes and that hair she wanted to run her fingers through. And what about that mouth of his? She simply could not stop longing to kiss him again. And then there were those broad, muscled shoulders, those calloused, talented hands.

The man was pure temptation, up close and in person.

"It was just a natural thing," Derek said, and she had no idea what he was talking about. She'd forgotten the question she had just asked him.

Not that it mattered, as long as she could continue to stare up at him, continue to feel this beautiful longing that she would never do anything about.

Uh-uh. No way. Not a chance. Forget about it.

"Neighbors helping neighbors," he said. "When he and Eva moved into the farmhouse, I dropped by to help them get settled in." Right. Luke. She'd asked him about Luke. "There were a lot of fences down on this place. I helped with that. And over at the Circle D, when some of our calves wandered off in a freak spring blizzard, Luke brought Bailey and helped me and my brother Eli and a couple of our cousins track them through the storm." He stared down at her, right into her eyes now.

She wished he would go on like that, just standing there looking at her, for a lifetime. Or two.

"Luke and me," he went on thoughtfully, "we just get along. He had a rough time, back when his parents died, but he came through it strong, you know? He's a man you can count on." Derek chuckled, a warm, rueful sound. "And besides, if I'm his best man, he doesn't have to choose between his brothers."

She laughed, too. "Well, yeah. There's that. Same thing with Eva. She chose me. So, her sisters and sisters-in-law can all be bridesmaids equally. Plus, she's been trying to get me back to town for thirteen years now. She kind of pulled out all the stops when she started in on me to be her maid of honor. Calla and Delphine put the pressure on, too. They were relentless, those three."

"Worked, didn't it?" His voice was low and rough, like they were sharing a secret, just the two of them. "Eva's a woman who knows what she wants and never quits until she gets it."

"I think she's matchmaking us," Amy said, the words just kind of popping out without permission from her brain.

One corner of that impossibly sexy mouth of his quirked up. "You think so, huh?"

Her cheeks felt so hot, burning red. "I… don't know why I said that."

"Yeah, you do." It was there in his eyes now, clear as day. He knew what she was up to, that she was trying to keep him there though it was past time for him to go.

And still, she longed simply to ask him to sit back down beside her, to talk to her, soft and low, about any old subject that wandered into his mind. She didn't care what they said.

She just wanted him near.

Good gravy, what was *wrong* with her? Enough of this reckless foolishness.

She rose.

He didn't back up, though.

They ended up mere inches apart. If she took a deep breath, her breasts would just about brush his hard chest.

And oh, the warmth of him, the strength and height of him.

The scent of him, of pine and leather.

Everything about him seemed to reach for her, to wrap around her, to reel her in.

And then he did reach for her. He hooked an arm around her waist. She let out a sharp gasp of mingled alarm and delight as he hauled her up tight against him, her breasts to his chest, her thighs pressed to his thighs—and oh, she could feel him, feel the evidence of his desire for her pressed to her belly.

Talk about intimate. "I..."

He bent a fraction closer. "You...?" It was a taunt. His eyes gleamed, so green and deep.

She pressed her lips into a thin, hard line. "You're mocking me." It came out barely a whisper. She was too breathless to give the words much sound.

"Yes, I am. And you're teasing me."

"No..."

"Miss Wainwright." He made a chiding sound. "Don't make me call you a liar. Besides, you know what?"

"What?"

"If you want to tease me, you go right on ahead. I don't mind at all." Derek pulled her closer.

Really, that shouldn't have been physically possible. She was already plastered against the front of him.

But he managed it anyway. He pulled her closer and she felt him even more acutely. Her whole body yearned. Yearned for the innocent passion they'd once shared. And not only that. She yearned for the man he was now, too.

Somehow, her hands had come to rest against his chest. Beneath his soft cotton shirt, she could feel the sculpted muscles, the fierce beating of his heart.

Dear God, she had loved him.

And there was no denying how very much she still wanted him.

There was just something about him that called to her so deeply. Some impossible power he had that made her burn for him even after all these long years.

He said a bad word, low, guttural. His head dipped closer…

And then, at last, his beautiful mouth touched hers.

Chapter 5

They were kissing.

Again.

After promising each other that wasn't going to happen.

Well, it *was* happening. And it was spectacular.

With a soft cry, she slid her hands up over those rock-like shoulders. She opened her mouth and he dipped his tongue in. Her grasping fingers threaded up into that sexy, messy hair of his.

"Amy. Amy," he said her name twice, breathing it into her mouth as he kissed her, lifting his head a fraction, just long enough to slant his kiss the other way.

She didn't say anything. She *couldn't* say anything. She was drowning in him, going down for the third time and loving it. She could kiss him forever, on into the next millennium, kiss him and kiss him and never, ever stop.

But then *he* stopped.

Abruptly.

He took her by the shoulders, ripped his mouth from hers and set her away. "No." His green eyes were like a stormy sea now.

She blinked. "No?"

"We need to stop doing this."

Her mind felt so thick and slow. Her body ached to have his arms wrapped around her again. "Doing...?"

He raked his hand back over his hair, smoothing it. Not that smoothing it did any good. His hair just flopped back over his forehead all over again. "Do I really have to spell it out for you? We've got to stop pretending we're not going to put our hands on each other— and then doing it anyway. It's messing with my head, you know? *Both* heads, as a matter of fact."

She almost laughed, but slapped her hand over her mouth just in time to stop herself— after which she felt thoroughly foolish. Letting her hand drop to her side, she nodded. "Okay. I get it. I'm... Look, I'm sorry. Okay?"

He took another step back from her. "I'm not blaming you, not any more than I'm blaming myself. We're both at fault. It's...what we do to each other."

She sucked in another shaky breath. "Yeah. It's crazy, huh? I mean, for me it's still the same. The, um, feeling I have for you. It's strong." She could not believe what she was admitting, but at the same time, it felt good, right, to lay it out there the way it really was for her. "Even after everything we went through, after all these years, I still feel it so powerfully for you. I was so scared, that first day, when you came here to the farmhouse. I thought I would shatter into a million pieces just at the sight of you. And I almost did."

He looked so young suddenly, his eyes almost hopeful. "Yeah?"

"Yeah."

"You tell me now, Amy Wainwright. Are you with anyone, back there in Boulder?"

"No, I'm not. I promise you. There's no one. What about you?"

A low, rough chuckle escaped him. "Like you even have to ask. It's Rust Creek Falls. If

I had a girl, you'd have heard all about it from at least ten different sources by now."

She did laugh then. "Eva, first of all."

"You got that right." His eyes grew serious again and his mouth was a flat line. "You lookin' for a little summer fun with an old flame, is that it?"

She wanted to cry suddenly. "Don't say that. You're so much more than just an old flame to me." *You're the father of the child I never had. My husband. For a while.*

He rubbed the back of his neck again. "I don't know."

Could he be any less clear? "You don't know what?"

"What you want from me, where you're going with this."

She put her hands out to the sides, palms up. "Where are *you* going? And why is it that I'm supposed to have all the answers?"

He didn't say, *You started it.* But he was thinking it. She could see it in his eyes, in the hard set to his square jaw. "I want you, too," he said at last. "It's strong. Really strong."

Her pulse pounded harder. She felt it beating in her neck as a pleasured flush flooded upward over her cheeks. "Well, then…" Seriously? She could not believe what she was about to suggest. "Why don't we just go with it?" She thought about Eva's advice Sunday morning. "Just kind of see where it takes us?"

He wasn't buying. "What if where it takes us is only back to heartbreak all over again?"

So much for putting herself out there. "Here we go again. I know that look on your face, Derek Dalton. You've suddenly got a fence to fix or a poor, lost calf you need to track down and rescue."

"That's right." He scooped his hat off the tack hanger and set it on his head. "I should get going."

Okay, now he was just plain pissing her off. "All of a sudden, I find I am tempted to start making chicken noises."

"You just need to think it over, okay? Think it over, and I will, too. But right now, I really have to go."

Derek did think it over. All the next day and the day after that.

Amy was pretty much all he thought about. Those big, honest eyes. The taste of her mouth and her soft, curvy body pressed up tight to his. The lemony smell of her hair. And the brave things she'd said.

"I still feel it so powerfully for you."

"You're so much more than just an old flame to me."

"Why don't we just go with it? Just kind of see where it takes us?"

He injured himself twice at the shop, punched a hole in his thumb tooling a set of saddlebags and took a slice out of his index finger cutting leather for another project. Blood all over. What a mess.

All because he couldn't keep his mind on the job. It was just like in high school, his brain focused on Amy all the time, the rest of the world receding into the background.

He knew, over the years, that some people judged him for being one of those guys who played it fast and easy, never sticking with one girl very long.

But no other girl was Amy. So, what was the point of starting anything too heavy? He kept things casual, moving on whenever a girl acted like she might get serious. He'd never been out to hurt anyone. He just wanted a good time on a Friday night.

A good time and maybe not to feel so alone for a while.

Lots of girls felt the same way he had. They weren't looking to settle down.

Now, though?

Well, he was over thirty. A different girl every weekend just kind of made him feel tired. Bailey Stockton might claim to admire him for never settling down, but Bailey was no kid, either. At some point almost every man—and woman, too, he would bet—wanted more than a stranger to take home at closing time.

Amy.

She still cranked his chain in a really big way. But she'd be leaving at the end of the month, going back to her own life. And his life was here.

It just seemed stupid to get anything going with her, stupid and a clear invitation to heartbreak.

By Friday, she hadn't called. What did that mean? She'd found the last few things they needed for the party? Or she'd changed her mind about wanting to "go with it," to "see where it takes us."

Whatever it meant, she hadn't gotten in touch.

And he needed to stop thinking about her.

That made him laugh—and not in a happy way. Stop thinking about her? To stop breathing would be easier.

"You all right?" Collin asked him Friday evening as they were closing up.

He gave his friend and business partner a wry grin and held up his bandaged hand—two small bandages, actually. One on his thumb and the other on his cut index finger. "What? All the blood scared you?"

"You do seem kind of distracted," Collin said mildly. He clapped Derek on the shoulder. "Why don't you come on up the mountain with me? Willa's making pot roast."

"'Night!" Ned called as went out the door. "See you guys Monday."

Derek waved at Ned and said to Collin, "I hate to pass up the best pot roast in Montana, but I told Luke I'd meet him and the boys for happy hour at the Ace. How about joining us?"

"Thanks, but I gotta get home."

They walked out together, Derek trying not to be jealous of an old friend who used to be considered a world-class heartbreaker, all settled down now with a wife and son he couldn't wait to get home to.

In the master bathroom upstairs at Sunshine Farm, Eva touched up her blusher and fluffed her blond hair.

Amy, leaning in the open doorway behind her, asked, "Are you sure about this? The guys might not be too happy about us crashing their happy hour two weeks running."

Eva giggled like a schoolgirl and leaned in closer to the mirror to put on her lipstick. "Of course they'll be happy." She smoothed on a glossy petal-pink shade. "They'd better be. Because I'm thinking we need to make this a Friday tradition." Eva had invited half the women in town to join them in crashing the guys' happy hour. She capped the lipstick. "Now, get over here." She wiggled her fingers back over her shoulder at Amy, who stepped up beside her. Eva hooked an arm around her waist. They grinned together at their reflections.

Amy said, "You look amazing."

Eva beamed. "And you look just beautiful."

Tonight, Amy wore a short red dress with a flirty hem that left her shoulders bare, and her favorite red-tooled cowboy boots. She'd spent way more time on her hair and makeup than a certain obstinate cowboy deserved. But she did have her pride and she liked to look her best. "You ready?" She kept her smile, though every time she thought of Derek, she wanted to pitch a world-class hissy fit.

Eva glanced at the small clock on the bathroom counter. "Yikes! We'd better get moving. Our girls will wonder what happened to us."

* * *

The Ace's dirt parking lot was packed. Amy let Eva out under the flickering neon sign at the entrance and drove around for ten minutes until finally an old guy in a battered pickup pulled out and left a free space. She parked and primped a little, and then got out and headed for the front door.

With every step she took, her hopeless heart knocked harder against her rib cage. Her blood seemed to hum through her veins and her stomach was a big ball of nerves.

All because he hadn't called and she hadn't called and they'd left it all open-ended last Tuesday night—or rather, *he* had. Telling her to "think it over."

Saying he would think it over, too.

Think it over?

After she'd gone and put her heart right out there, as good as begging him to be with her for the rest of the month, that was all she got? She'd tried so hard to be honest and forthright with him.

And in return, he'd said to think about it— oh, and by the way, he had to go.

Inside the Ace, the music was loud, the dance floor packed. Eva and five other women, friends and family, had joined the group of men at the three large pushed-together tables near the long mahogany bar.

Derek was there, all right, looking like every cowgirl's fantasy in a worn plaid shirt and a straw Resistol. The table blocked her view of his long, strong legs clad in denim and his brown cowboy boots, but she knew he would be wearing them, whether he'd spent his day at the saddlery or working cattle on the Circle D.

A waitress she'd never seen before stood at his shoulder with a tray full of empties. She was really pretty, with a lush, curvy figure and long platinum hair.

She bent close to Derek and whispered something in his ear. He said something in reply. Really, he wasn't flirting with her. He didn't lean close to her and his smile was only casually friendly.

Amy hated them both anyway. Just on principle. Because he'd told her to "think it over." And because why did he have to be the guy every pretty woman wanted to get to know a whole lot better?

The waitress threw back her platinum head and let out a musical laugh as she turned and strutted to the bar.

Derek spotted Amy then, where she stood watching on the far side of the dance floor. His eyes seemed to burn into hers. He reached out, hooked the seat of an empty chair at the next table over and eased it in between his chair and Bailey's beside him. Then he patted the seat.

As if she was going to trot right over there and sit next to him just because he patted a chair.

Eva caught sight of her. "Amy! There you are!" She waved madly.

Amy ordered her legs to start moving. She marched straight to Eva, who sat between Luke and Viv Shuster on a long bench seat.

"Got room for me?" Amy asked.

"You bet." Viv scooted closer to her fiancé, Cole Dalton, on her other side. As Eva had explained it to Amy, Cole had come to town last year with his brothers and his dad for a fresh start after the family had lost everything in a tragic fire. The dark-haired cowboy was clearly head-over-heels for the wedding planner. He hooked an arm across Viv's shoulders and drew her closer still.

Amy was glad for them. She was glad for all the happy couples in Rust Creek Falls. Too bad love hadn't worked out so well for her, she thought grumpily as she took the vacant space Viv had left for her. Across the table, she could just *feel* Derek scowling at her.

Not that she was going to look at him again. He could just sit there with that empty chair and wait for that waitress to come whisper a few more sweet nothings in his ear for all Amy cared.

There were pitchers of beer already on the table. Eva grabbed a clean glass and poured one for Amy.

"Raise your glasses, everyone," Eva instructed. When the glasses went up, she offered, "To love and happy hour."

The toast echoed around the table. Everybody drank and Eva and Luke shared a kiss, after which Luke took her hand and led her out to the dance floor. Everybody else at the table seemed to think that was a great idea. Most of them, including Cole and Viv, got up to dance. Bailey stayed behind. Bella and Hudson Jones, too.

Across the table, Derek asked, "Dance with me, Amy?"

She pretended she didn't hear him. And when a tall, skinny cowboy asked her dance, she got up and two-stepped with him for all she was worth. Not once did she allow herself to glance at the table or look around to see what Derek "The Lady-Killer" Dalton might be doing.

When the tall cowboy took her back to her seat, she gave him a big smile as he thanked her for the dance. She turned to sit down and her eyes lit on Derek—and that waitress. She was bending close to him as she set a shot glass full of amber liquid in front of him.

Amy shouldn't have looked.

But she did look. And that waitress had some serious cleavage, which she was sticking right in Derek's face.

That did it. There was no point in this.

None at all.

Amy spoke to Bailey. "I think I'm going to take off. Tell Eva I'm fine. I know she can hitch a ride home with Luke."

Bailey opened his mouth to say something, but then seemed to think better of it, whatever it was. He swallowed and nodded. "Sure thing, Amy. Drive safe."

"Thanks, Bailey." She turned and got moving, her cowboy boots tapping the wood floor swift and sharp, as she skirted the dance area on the way to the exit.

She shoved through to the wide porch in front. Outside, it was still daylight, though the sun had slipped close to the mountains. She ran down the stairs and around to the still-full parking lot.

Almost at her car, she heard swift footsteps behind her.

"Come on, Amy." *Derek*. He had followed her. "Damn it, wait up!"

She kept going, down the dirt aisle between the two rows of cars, feeling hurt and frustrated and angry.

And way too relieved that he'd come after her.

She reached her Audi and marched to the driver's door.

"Amy!"

"Fine," she muttered under her breath to no one in particular. Folding her arms hard under her breasts, she leaned back against the side of the car as he turned from the aisle and strode toward her. "What?" she demanded.

He stopped, whipped off his hat and rubbed the back of his neck. "Look. I got nothing going on with Myra. She flirts. She gets bigger tips that way."

"Oh, her name is Myra, is it?"

"It's no secret. It's on her name tag."

She almost started in on him about the proximity of Myra's cleavage to his face. But that would be tacky. "We both know that Myra's not the issue, okay?"

"Amy, it doesn't look to me like anything

is 'okay' between us right at this moment..."
His voice trailed off. She could hear laughter
and voices a couple of aisles over—and nearer
to where they stood, too—customers on their
way in and out of the Ace. "We're a block and
a half from the saddlery. Would you meet me
there? We can talk in private."

"I don't know if that's a good idea."

"Please." He said it softly, sincerely. Like it
was really important to him. Like he wouldn't
be able to bear it if they didn't work this out.

"Fine," she said tightly. "I'll meet you at the
saddlery." He just stood there, looking at her.
"What?" she demanded.

"When a woman says 'fine' like that, a man
has doubts that anything is fine in any way."

"Your point being?"

"You're not going to take off again, are you?"

"I said I would be there."

"All right. I'll see you in ten minutes, then."

By the time Derek arrived at the shop, Amy
was already there. He parked in the space next
to her as she got out of her car and ran up the
steps.

At the door, she stepped back and wrapped
her arms around herself, like he might contami-
nate her if she happened to actually touch him.

He could think of a few snide remarks he might make about now. But that would get them nowhere. He kept his mouth shut as he stuck his key in the lock and stepped past the threshold to turn off the alarm and switch on the lights.

"Come on in. There's a table and chairs in back. We can make coffee, if you want some." He led the way through the shop to the make-shift lounge area. Once through the open door, he suggested, "Have a seat."

She pulled out a vinyl-covered chair at the scratched-up laminate table and sat down.

He was already sticking a pod in the coffee maker. "You want some coffee?"

"Sure," she said, her mouth pinched, as if even the thought of drinking his coffee was annoying her. "Thanks," she added sourly.

He brewed a cup for each of them, took the seat across from her and pushed one of the mugs in her direction. "There's sugar. And creamer." Way back in ancient history, she liked both. He pushed the container of pack-ets her way, too.

And then he just sat there, hardly knowing where to start. He drank the coffee he really didn't want as he watched her add a packet of sugar and creamer to her mug and take a cautious sip.

They shouldn't be here. Shouldn't be doing this.

And yet, if she got up and tried to leave right now, he would do whatever he had to do to convince her to stay.

Was he messed up over this woman or what?

Stupid question with an obvious answer.

Finally, she spoke. "Okay. I'm here. What did you want to say to me?"

Damned if he knew. "I just don't see why you're so mad at me. You said it's not about Myra."

"And it's not. It's just…it's everything, Derek. All these years and how much you hurt me and now it seems to me like you're just messing with me all over again."

Now, that was just wrong. "*I'm* messing with *you*? What are you talking about? How am I messing with you?"

"One minute you act like we're completely over and done, the next you're bringing a picnic, showing me around here in the saddlery, kissing me. Twice."

He was in midsip when she mentioned those kisses, and the scornful way she spoke of them made him mad enough that he plunked his mug down hard. Hot liquid splashed on his hand. He swore under his breath as he whipped a paper towel from the roll in the center of the table and wiped up the spill. "Next you'll be claiming you didn't kiss me back."

She huffed out a furious breath. "That is completely and totally not in any way the point. Yes, I kissed you back. Yes, I loved that picnic and the tour you gave me here. I loved every minute I've spent with you this last week."

How did she do that? Drive him crazy one minute, and the next say something that had all his wounded fury draining right out of him. Carefully, he set the wadded ball of paper towel beside his mug. "You did?"

"Yes, I did. I even started thinking that maybe we could have a little something special together, that we could leave the past *in* the past and be together right now."

"Amy, I—"

She whipped up a hand. "Wait." And then she sat back in the chair and folded her arms hard across her middle. "Think back. What did you say when I suggested we see where this feeling between us might take us?" He would have answered. He even opened his mouth to do so, but she just rolled right on. "I'll tell you what you said. You said that I ought to think about it. You said that you would be thinking, too. Well, you know what? I don't believe you, Derek. I don't think you thought about it one bit since Tuesday night. Uh-uh. More likely you've spent all this time purposely *not* thinking about it, planning on going out this weekend and finding yourself some other girl, some *new* girl you don't have any baggage with."

"That's bull. I'm not looking for any new girl. And I did think about it—about you and me and seeing where it would take us. It's *all* I thought about." He lifted his left hand and wiggled the bandaged digits at her. "I practically cut all my fingers off thinking about it."

"Oh, please. As if you cut yourself because you were so wrapped up in pining for me."

"That is exactly what I did."

For a moment, her eyes softened and her mouth relaxed. But then she snapped right back to hissy-fit mode. "You just don't get it," she accused.

He threw up both hands. "And you're not listening to me."

She fumed at him, tapping her fingers on her crossed arms. "It took me forever to accept that you were never coming after me. Took me driving all the way back here from Boulder nine years ago, daring to hope that just maybe

I might get a chance to talk to you. Took me stopping in at the Ace and chatting up the bartender, who told me all about what a player you were, how it was one girl after another with you. About the cute cowgirl you'd met there at the Ace the weekend before, how you danced every dance with her and left with her at closing time, how word in town was that you were off at the Missoula Stampede with her right that very moment."

He vaguely remembered the cowgirl in question, but a long-ago hookup wasn't what had him sitting up straight in his chair. "Wait. Are you serious? You came back?"

She scrunched her eyes tight and let out a moan. "Yeah. I came back and you were off with some other girl and I realized I needed to accept that you had moved on and to start finding a way to move on myself."

He pushed his chair back. "Amy..."

She glared at him as he stood. "What are we doing here? What is the point of this?"

Her words were not the least bit encouraging. But...she'd come back. She'd actually come back.

And he'd never even known.

"Amy..." He rounded the table. He just couldn't stop himself.

When he stood by her chair, she stared up at him defiantly. "Yeah, I came back. So what? I came back and you were with another girl."

"Amy, I didn't know. I never had a clue..."

"Don't do that, okay? Don't look at me like I'm so important to you. We both know that's just not true."

"But you are important. Always were, always will be."

She made a little scoffing sound. "Yeah, right."

He needed to prove it, needed her to know that he'd missed her, too. So, he went ahead and confessed, "I tried to find you, too. I went to Boulder, Amy. Like a lovesick fool, I went to CU looking for you."

Her eyes got wide and her pinched-up mouth went soft and full again. "You did?"

His chest felt constricted. His throat, too. "It was that first year after you left, in the early spring. I didn't know what the hell I was doing, how to go about getting in touch with you. I tried your old cell number. Some stranger answered, said it was his number now. I was afraid to ask the Armstrongs or someone who might know how to reach you. Afraid they wouldn't tell me. Afraid they'd tell *you* and you would refuse to see me. And there was zero access to social media around here at the time. I couldn't exactly look you up on Facebook."

She gazed at him across the table, her mouth softly parted, her eyes all dewy and so bright. "But you drove to Colorado anyway, to try and find me?"

"I did, yeah. I missed you so much. I couldn't stand it anymore. Drove all night and half the next day. It was snowing on and off, sometimes snowing hard, but I kept going. I had this idea that if you saw me, saw my face, knew how much I'd missed you, you'd maybe decide you couldn't live without me, either."

"But you never showed up."

"Yeah, I did. I mean, I made it to Boulder, anyway, to the main CU campus. I parked and went in to the administration building."

"And?"

"They wouldn't tell me squat. Turned out they have rules about that," he laughed, but it was a dry sound with very little humor in it. "I could've been a stalker or something. Hell, after driving fifteen hours in near-blizzard conditions, I probably *looked* like a stalker."

"Derek." Her eyes gleamed, wet now with unshed tears. "I'm so sorry. I didn't know."

He laughed again, humorless as the time

before. "Pretty hard for you to know when I didn't tell a soul."

"What did you do then?"

"I went back to my truck and considered pulling out all the stops, paying a visit to your parents' house."

"You had my parents' address?"

He shrugged. "They were easy. I found a phone book. They were listed. But school was in session and I was reasonably sure you wouldn't be at your folks' house. That meant I'd be dealing with your mom and dad. They'd never been my biggest fans, your dad especially, though he was polite enough that last day."

"At the motel in Kalispell, you mean?"

He debated just going ahead and telling her the whole truth about that day. But what good would that do anyone, really? "Yeah. At the motel."

She pushed back her chair and stood. "You're such a bad liar."

He put up both hands and backed up a step. "I'm not—"

"Don't say it. I didn't believe you the first time, so there's no point in lying to me again." She shook her head. "I always wondered how my dad knew to follow us from the Armstrong house. I asked him about it more than once.

He always just said he'd tried dropping by the Armstrongs' and he saw us drive away."

"It's ancient history, Amy."

She wouldn't leave it alone. "He got to you, didn't he? He went to find you at the Circle D and then he followed you to the Armstrongs' house and when you picked me up, he trailed both of us to Kalispell."

Derek couldn't believe he'd put himself in the position of defending Jack Wainwright. But at this point, she wouldn't believe him anyway if he insisted on keeping the truth from her. They were clearing the air, after all. Letting all their sad little secrets out of the closets.

"All right. Yeah. Your dad showed up at the ranch. He was worried sick about you. And I have to say, even though I didn't like him any more than he liked me, I knew he loved you and wanted the best for you. He was also no fool. He didn't threaten me or talk down to me. He took hat in hand, said he knew I loved you, said that you had a bright future in front of you and why would a man who loved you want to steal that future out from under you? He said he just wanted me to think about letting you go."

"Oh, Derek," she cried. "Why didn't you just tell me that you'd talked to him?"

"I thought about it, about us, about what your dad had said. I thought about it all the way from the Armstrong house to our dingy little honeymoon suite at that crappy motel. And the more I thought it over, the more certain I was that if I told you your dad had come looking for me, you'd just get mad at him. You'd dig in your heels and not admit that he was right."

She pressed her lips together. "I'm mad at him right now. He went behind my back and he never came clean to me about what he did."

"Amy, it's really old news."

"Still…"

"It's old news and he did it because he loved you."

"Yeah, well. Next time I see him, I'll tell him I know the truth now and I don't appreciate the way he lied to me."

"That's your call."

"Oh, yes, it is—and we're not finished talking about the day you drove to Colorado to try to l find me at CU. Did you go see my parents that day?" Her eyes got stormy. "Because if you did, they never said a word to me about that, either."

"Settle down."

"Then answer the question, please." Her voice was clipped, tight.

"No, I didn't go to see your parents. I chickened out and just went home."

"Oh," she said, her outrage fading. "I see."

"And what did *you* do, after that bartender told you I was off in Missoula with some other girl?"

She scanned his face as though memorizing it. "Same as you. I chickened out and went home."

For a few seconds that seemed to last forever and a day, they just stood there, mere inches between them, gazes locked, neither even breathing.

And then he reached out.

And she stepped forward.

His arms went around her. She rested her head against his shoulder. He gathered her closer. Never would he get enough of the perfect feel of her in his arms.

When she finally looked up, she went on tiptoe and brushed a quick kiss on his chin. "Aren't we a pair?"

They laughed together. And he agreed, "Yeah. A matched set, no doubt about it."

"You really cut your hand thinking about me?"

"I did."

"Let me see." When he held up his injured

fingers, she took them and kissed the bandaged spots. "Be more careful," she chided.

"Great advice." Though now that he was here, alone with her, the last thing he wanted was to be careful.

"Derek, I…" Those big hazel eyes searched his face.

"Yeah?"

"I still want to be with you. I want to spend every minute I can with you until the wedding. I don't know what will happen, really. Maybe you and I aren't meant for forever. But you told me to think about it and I have. And the answer's still the same. I want to be with you, to get to know you, to know the man you are now."

He wanted that, too—to know the Amy she was now—so damn much.

Yeah, she scared the hell out of him. She could hurt him so deep if he let her get too close. She'd probably break his heart all over again.

Too bad it was too late to walk away untouched. Somehow, she'd gone and worked her way back under his skin—or maybe she'd never left.

He wanted her so bad it hurt.

"It's only two weeks and a day till the wedding now," she said. "I would like to spend a lot of that time with you. I would like us to commit to being exclusive till the wedding."

She would like that? He would *love* it. "Exclusive, huh?"

"That's right. Yes or no? Can you give up the other women at least for the next fifteen days?"

"Amy, let me clear this up for you once and for all. There *are* no other women. Yes, I've been one of those guys who never sticks around for breakfast the morning after, but not in the past few years. I haven't been with anyone in a little over eight months and that was an actual relationship. Her name is Angela Bishop. She owns a diner in Kalispell." He added, with more sarcasm than was probably called for, "We went on dates and everything."

She scrunched up her eyebrows at him, an expression he recognized as concern for him. "What happened?"

"With Angela? Not enough. I mean, she liked me and I liked her and we had a good time together, but at a certain point we both realized it wasn't going anywhere. We broke up. End of story. So, would you please stop assuming I'm spending all my free time chasing women?"

She gave a slow, solemn nod. "Will do. I promise. And I'm sorry to have, um, made assumptions about you."

"You're forgiven. Now, about the next two weeks…"

She drew her shoulders back. "I would like to be with you."

"Got that."

"And to keep what we have just between the two of us. Because nobody else has to know."

Did that bother him? Not really. Rust Creek Falls was a very small town. People looked out for each other, but they also got way too interested in each others' activities. He could do without them all talking about him and Amy.

She went on, "It's partly to keep everyone out of our business. I mean, it's only two weeks and who knows what will happen? And until *we* know where we're going together, there's no reason to share what we have with the rest of the world. Also, I think it's important to keep the focus on Eva and Luke, where it belongs right now. We'll say we're just friends…" Her cheeks were pink and her eyes so wide and hopeful. "I mean, for the next two weeks, we could make time for each other and not date other people. And I'm hoping there could be, um, benefits if it works out that way. That's all I'm really asking. Would that work for you?"

He hid a grin. "I think I could manage it."

A little snort of laughter escaped her. "Stop joking. This is serious."

He put on his most somber expression. "Just friends, then. Friends who spend a lot of time together and don't go out with other people. Friends with possible secret benefits?"

"Well, yeah. I mean, you think?" She folded her upper lip between her teeth and nibbled on it. The sight was equal parts innocent and sexy. He wanted to grab her and kiss her, unwrap her like the best gift ever, get going on those benefits, secret or otherwise…

But he knew her, even with all the empty years away from her. She wasn't ready yet. And if it happened for them again—*when* it happened—he wanted it to be right.

"Is that too crazy?" Her voice was barely a whisper. "Am I totally on the wrong track here? Would you agree to something like that?" She stared up at him, anxious and adorable. "Derek, you have to tell me what you think."

"I do, huh?"

"Derek!" She whipped up a hand and batted his shoulder.

He caught her fingers before she could pull them away. "Hold on a minute."

"What are you doing?"

"I'll show you. But first, I think you should come closer."

Just like a woman, she hung back. "But I—"

"Closer." He laid her hand, palm flat, on his shoulder. "Don't move that hand." For that, he got an eye roll, but her palm stayed where he'd put it. It felt good there. It felt right. He almost let himself imagine a lifetime's worth of her soft hands touching him. But he didn't, not quite. No reason to get too carried away here. "Now, give me the other one."

"But, Derek, what do you—"

"Come on. Humor me." She offered her hand cautiously. He took it, opened her fingers and rested it on his other shoulder. "There."

She looked deliciously doubtful. "Now what?"

He clasped her waist. "It feels good." His voice came out gruff though he hadn't really meant it to. "It feels good to have your hands on me. To touch you. Nothing ever felt as good as touching you, Amy."

"Derek," she whispered, and somehow managed to put a thousand tender meanings into just saying his name.

"Amy." He swooped down and claimed himself a quick, sweet kiss, after which he announced, "I want to be with you, too. Exclusive secret friends, just the way you described it. With benefits—maybe. When the time is right."

She wrinkled her beautiful nose at him. "You're not just messing with me? You really mean it? You won't change your mind and stay away from me for days on end?"

He should have sense enough to let that stand. But he'd never had much sense around her. "It was only two days—okay, three if you count today."

She tipped her head to the side and slanted him a narrow-eyed look. "You *were* staying away, though, weren't you?"

"I was thinking it over, as we agreed."

She blew out a hard breath. "I can see this is an argument you're never going to let me win."

"You're right. I'm not. I'm also not messing with you. I meant what I said. I've thought it through and, if you agree, I won't be keeping my distance anymore. I want to be with you, too. For the next two weeks, you and me."

"And if either of us is too busy or whatever and we can't be together, we'll keep in communication?" Her eyes were almost golden right then. Golden and shining.

"Yeah," he said. "We'll be together, be honest with each other, see where it takes us."

"Starting right this minute." She slid those

soft hands up around his neck. Her cool fingers stroked the short hair at his nape. "Kiss me again."

He couldn't comply fast enough. Her lips were so soft and sweet. And her body fit against him as if she was born to be his. She opened for him eagerly and he tasted her more deeply, savoring the warmth and wet beyond her parted lips.

And that time, when he lifted his head, she asked, "Are you still in the bunkhouse at the Circle D?"

He touched her hair, so silky and warm. For the next two weeks, he would touch her a lot. Touch her everywhere, he hoped—eventually. When the time was right. "I built my own place a few years back. My brothers and cousins pitched in to help me, along with some friends who work in construction. It's not a big place, not fancy, but it's mine, you know?"

"I would love to see it."

"Now?"

"Yes." Her smile took his breath away. "I'll text Eva to let her know that I'll be out late. And then I'll follow you home."

Chapter 6

Once they turned off the highway onto Circle D land, Derek led the way in his pickup along the winding dirt ranch road past the main house, the barn and the bunkhouse.

Amy followed him, bumping along, trying her best to avoid the ruts. They skirted a pretty, rolling meadow. The house stood on the far side of the meadow, with a big cottonwood in the front yard. Sided in natural wood, it had a long front porch and three gabled windows breaking up the roofline.

Derek circled the cottonwood and parked facing back toward the highway. She followed him around the tree and pulled to a stop behind him. It was about eight by then, still light out. But the sun had gone behind the mountains and the pale moon rode high in the blue expanse of the Montana sky, the orange fingers of sunset beginning to color the wisps of clouds above the crests of the distant peaks.

An almost-white Labrador retriever came down the front steps, tail wagging. Derek, already out of his pickup, stopped to greet the dog, who gazed at him adoringly as he scratched the ruff at the animal's neck.

Amy got out and shut her door. "I didn't know you had a dog."

"I don't. Meet Buster. He belongs to Willa and Collin, but every once in a while, he takes off down the mountain and comes here or goes to the Christensen place."

The Christensens were Willa's family. Actually, Willa and Collin were kind of an unexpected match: Willa the good-girl kindergarten teacher and Collin Traub, who never met a rule he wouldn't break. "I was surprised when Eva told me that Willa and Collin got married."

"So were a lot of people. They got together during the big flood." The flood had swept through Rust Creek Falls and the surrounding valley. Half the town had to be rebuilt afterward. "And now Collin and Willa have a son named Robbie and a dog who likes to wander." He grinned down at Buster.

"He's a beautiful dog." Buster seemed to preen at her praise. He sat back on his haunches and stared up at her expectantly. She knelt to pet him.

"Watch out. He'll drool all over your dress."

"I don't mind." She scratched his head and let him swipe his big tongue across her cheek. "Why don't you have a dog of your own? Seems only right, now that you have your own place."

His gaze scanned her face, a look both slow and appreciative. "I'm at the saddlery half the time now. Wouldn't be fair to keep a dog cooped up there." He held down his hand to her. She took it, loving the warm, intimate feel of his fingers closing around hers. "Let me show you the house."

Buster trailing along in their wake, Derek led her up the steps. At the door, he ushered her in first. The dog slipped around them both and headed off down the hallway that opened up to what looked like a great room at the far end.

They stood in the small foyer area for a moment. She admired the handsome oak staircase accented with iron balusters and asked, "How many bedrooms are up there?"

"None right now. It's an unfinished attic. I

figure I can fix it up, divide it into bedrooms, even put in another bath if I ever need more living space."

If he ever needs more space...

Her mind went where it probably shouldn't—to the idea of Derek, married. Maybe with children.

Uh-uh. She blinked the thought away. It was too dangerous on too many levels.

"This way," he said.

He ushered her into the dining room, to the left of the entry and through there to the kitchen, breakfast nook, great room and two bedrooms. The furniture was basic, in a mishmash of styles.

"It's really nice," she said, "comfortable and inviting." There was even a big-screen TV above the natural stone fireplace.

He reached out and slid a hand under her hair, curving his strong, work-roughened fingers around the nape of her neck and pulling her in close to him. His lips brushed her cheek and his breath was warm in her ear. "You smell like heaven. Always did." An arrow of pure happiness darted straight through her heart at his whispered words. They shared a long, sweet kiss and then he lifted his head and captured her gaze. "Are you hungry?"

"A little."

At their feet, Buster whined and wagged his tail.

She leaned her head on Derek's shoulder. "I think you'd better feed Buster first."

He pressed his lips into her hair. It was an absolutely lovely moment and she let herself revel in it.

Too soon, he released her to fill one bowl with water and another with kibble. "Yeah," he replied to the question she hadn't even asked. "Buster stops by a lot and so I keep food on hand for him." He set the full bowls down and Buster went right to work gobbling his dinner. "I'd better let Collin know that his dog stopped by for dinner." Derek took out his phone and sent his friend a text.

When he stuck the phone back in his pocket, she said, "I want to help with the food."

"Works for me."

He made pasta with marinara sauce and Italian sausage. She tossed a quick salad with the lettuce and vegetables he had in the fridge, set the table and grated the parmesan.

Her phone buzzed with a text as they sat down to eat. She would have ignored it, but he said, "It could be important."

So, she checked. "It's Eva. She says we should have fun."

"Let me guess. There's a winky emoji followed by about ten hearts."

"I'm beginning to think you know her as well as I do."

He laughed. "Tell her I said hi."

As she typed a quick response, another text came in. She sent her reply to Eva and brought up the new message.

L.A. Noire. Tonight. Your house? I've got a nice Pinot Gris with your name on it.

She tapped out a quick reply. Sorry. Out of town for a few weeks.

Damn, woman. I was really in the mood to take you down.

Right. Like that's ever gonna happen.

Ping me.

Will do. Later.

She hit Send and glanced up to find Derek watching her. "A friend in Boulder. We play video games sometimes. He didn't know I was out of town."

Those green eyes were cool suddenly. "This friend got a name?"

"Jonas Baldwin." She picked up her fork again. "I met him in graduate school. We've stayed friends in a casual way." Derek just went on looking at her, his mouth a flat line. She thought of Myra, back at the Ace, and of how much she'd needed his reassurance that he had nothing going on with Myra. "Honestly, Derek. Jonas and I are in no way, shape or form, a thing and we never have been. We double-dated once—he took the girl he was dating at the time and I went with a friend of his. I see him maybe five or six times a year. He'll call and if I'm not doing anything, we get together, him and me and my Xbox One."

Derek just went on looking at her for several extremely uncomfortable seconds. Annoyance sizzled through her that he didn't believe her when she was telling the truth. He had no reason not to take her word for it—not to mention, he had zero right to be jealous. They'd only been exclusive for about two hours.

But then he asked, "Who wins?" and his mouth curved into that panty-melting grin.

Her heart lifted. "Are you kidding? I wipe the floor with him every time."

He tipped his beer at her. "Now, that's what I

wanted to hear." The doorbell chimed. "That'll be Collin looking for Buster." He got up and pushed his chair in. "Be right back. Come on, Buster." The dog followed him down the central hall.

Amy let them go—and then felt uncomfortable. As though she was hiding there in the kitchen. From Collin Traub, of all people. Back in high school, Derek was every girl's handsome heartthrob. Collin was the dangerous one, the forbidden fantasy, with his jet-black hair and dark, knowing eyes. Just as many girls dreamed of him as wanted Derek.

Not Amy. It had always been Derek for her.

And right now, what mattered was that she knew him, knew Collin, and even if she and Derek were keeping this thing just between them, the least she could do was show her face at the door and say hi to an old schoolmate.

She slid her napkin next to her half-finished plate, pushed back her chair and followed the sound of men's voices to the front door.

Collin, just outside the door with his dog waiting patiently at his feet, caught sight of her first. "Amy Wainwright." He gave Derek a strange, narrow-eyed look, then aimed his killer smile at her. "How you been?"

"Hi, Collin. I'm doing well, thanks."

As she stepped up beside him, Derek shot her a questioning frown, which she'd kind of expected after she'd made such a big deal back at the saddlery about the two of them keeping their relationship on the down low.

Amy shook Collin's hand. "Good to see you."

"Must be your Audi, then," he said, shooting another significant glance at Derek.

Derek grunted. "Why are we standing here at the door? Come on in. I've got a longneck with your name on it."

"Better not. I have to get back." But Collin stayed where he was and his gaze shifted her way again, his dark eyes watchful. "It's been a long time."

"Yeah." She rushed into the usual chitchat, the stuff you say to people you never knew all that well and haven't seen in more than a decade. "So, you and Willa Christensen, huh?"

"That's right."

"I always liked Willa—and I know this is long overdue, but congratulations, Collin."

"Thanks." Collin's guarded expression relaxed a little. "She really is the best thing that ever happened to me."

"And I understand you have a little boy—oh, and you're the mayor now, too?"

He smirked. "Never saw that coming, I'll bet."

"True." After all, Collin had been the classic high school bad boy. He partied hard, broke a lot of hearts, drove too fast and got in trouble with the sheriff more than once. "You never seemed like someone who would get into politics."

Collin laughed at that. "Talk about an understatement. Most of my life, not only would I never have considered running for public office, I never would have believed that anyone would vote for me."

"So, what changed?"

"I married Willa," he said with pride. "I had ideas for what I thought needed fixing around here and my wife decided I should step right up and make it happen."

"You're happy," Amy said softly, glad for him. "It's good to see how well things worked out for you."

"Can't complain."

Derek started to say something, but Collin went on before he got a word out. "What took you so long to come back to town?" He was looking faintly disapproving again.

"Long story," she said, and left it at that.

Collin's dark eyes seemed to look right through her. "I think I heard someone say you're here for the wedding?"

"I am." She rushed on. "It's been so good to see Eva, to get a chance to reconnect with old friends. Delphine and Calla and their families will be here next Friday. I can't wait to see them."

"And after the wedding, then what?" Collin didn't sound hostile, exactly. Just skeptical—and wary, too.

Derek muttered, "Come on, man."

Collin locked eyes with him and said almost gently, "It's a reasonable thing to ask."

Amy answered Collin's question, more or less. "I live in Boulder."

"So, a month in Montana *reconnecting* with old friends. Then back to real life." It was the truth, even if Collin Traub made it sound like something downright shady.

Before she could reply, Derek muttered, "Enough." He and Collin shared a look that seemed to speak volumes—about what, exactly, Amy couldn't be sure.

Collin took a step back. "You're right. I should get moving. See you Monday. Amy, you take care now."

"Thanks. You, too." She gave him a big smile. Because she really had nothing against Collin. No need to make an issue of his weirdly disapproving attitude.

Collin went down the steps, Buster at his heels, headed for the crew cab parked beside her SUV.

Derek shut the door.

She faced him. "Let me guess. Collin remembers that we used to be together in high school."

"Yeah." Derek headed to the kitchen. She fell in step behind him.

They took their seats at the table. He sipped his beer and she debated trying to go on as if the conversation with Collin hadn't happened.

He made the decision for her. "Go ahead. Ask me."

She took a fortifying sip of ice water and set the glass down with care. "How much does Collin know about you and me?"

He drank again. "That you were my girl and it ended when you moved away."

"That's all? He seemed a little too suspicious of me, like I did something bad to you."

"Maybe you're imagining things."

"Am I?"

He stared at her across the table for a few seconds that seemed to go on forever. And then he admitted, "The night I heard that you and your family had left for Colorado, I went out drinking."

"With Collin?"

"At some point, I met up with him. By then, I was really blasted. We ended up at this bonfire with a bunch of kids from Kalispell. I might've said a few stupid things to him and he might've gotten the idea that you ripped out my heart and chopped it into tiny pieces."

She had a strong urge to defend herself, to argue that he wasn't the only one who'd ended up with a ripped-out heart. But they'd been there, said all that—twice, as a matter of fact. No reason to hash it out all over again.

Instead, she asked, "So then, that night you got so drunk, you told him we'd been married?"

"No. I don't think so."

"You don't *know*?"

"Didn't I just say I got really drunk?" He glared at her. "In case you haven't heard, drunk people sometimes say and do things they later can't remember."

Did she blame him for being annoyed with this conversation? Not really. He had to be sick of rehashing the past. She certainly was. But she did want to understand Collin's attitude at the door. "So, you *might* have told him we were married, but you doubt it."

"That's right. I can't be absolutely sure of

what I said or didn't say. But if I'd slipped up and mentioned that we'd run off and gotten married, I'm thinking he'd have brought it up to me by now."

She poked at a slice of sausage with her fork. "He seems like he's a really good friend to you. A true friend, you know?"

"Look." His voice was hard. "Just tell me. Are you pissed off that I might have told Collin you married me once?"

"No. If you did tell him, I understand why."

"You sure?"

"Positive. I mean, it was a bad time. You probably needed to talk to someone and Collin's your friend." She thought of Eva. Of Delphine and Calla. They were her true friends, yet she'd never told them the truth about the past. Guilt jabbed at her, that she'd kept the secret for so long, that she would probably go right on keeping it. "At the door just now, Collin asked about my car. What was he getting at?"

"Before you decided to come say hi to him, he asked if I had company. I said, just a friend. Wasn't that what I was supposed to say?"

"I'm not criticizing you, Derek. I'm only trying to understand why he seemed suspicious of me—and protective of you."

"Yeah, well, you could have avoided all that by staying in here until I got rid of him."

She swallowed. Hard. He had a good point and she needed to explain herself. "It seemed tacky somehow, you know? To hide in the kitchen while you sent away someone we both went to school with."

"Amy, it's what you asked for. To be 'secretly, exclusively together.' Am I right?" And then he added, under his breath, "Whatever the hell all that even means."

She set down her fork with care. "You're upset with me."

"Yeah. You've got me all turned around here. You say we're keeping what we're doing a secret. Then you come strolling down the hall to greet Collin at the door after I've tried to cover for your being here. I don't know what you want."

"I guess I didn't think it through, when I proposed how we would be together. I just meant we wouldn't explain ourselves, okay?"

His strong jaw was set. "Uh-uh. Still don't get it."

"Well, I mean when we're together, we're together and people are going to see that. I don't want us to lie."

"Yeah, you do. You want us to lie and say

we're just friends when we're more than friends and we always will be, whether we move on to benefits or not."

We always will be.

Her heart pounded harder and her skin felt too tight. He was right, and she knew it. And it made her ridiculously glad—that after more than a decade apart, she was still important to him.

She tried again to explain herself. "I only meant that we could just skip the PDAs and the declarations of our relationship, or whatever. We can just tell everyone we're friends and leave it at that. I didn't mean we would hide or pretend I'm not at your house when I am."

He pushed his plate away. "Okay. No PDAs and we tell everyone we're friends. And when your car's parked outside my house all night, we just say you stayed over and let them think whatever they want to think."

"Yes. That's it. Exactly."

"So, there is no secret, really. There are just zero explanations."

"Yeah. Is that wrong somehow, Derek?"

"We might as well get real about this. If we're not keeping our getting together a secret, they're going to talk anyway. In case you didn't notice, it's Rust Creek Falls."

"I'm just saying that this is none of their business. *We're* none of their business. It's just between us and they can talk all they want, but we'll just ignore them." He didn't reply so she pressed him. "I'll ask again, do you think that not explaining ourselves to other people is wrong?"

"No, I don't think it's wrong. And I do want to be with you, however we can make that work." He stared across the table in her general direction, but he wasn't really meeting her eyes.

"Well, okay, then." She waited for him to look directly at her so that she could try a coaxing smile.

But he only lowered his gaze and turned his empty beer bottle in a slow circle, staring at it as though deep in thought. "You realize I said '*When* your car's parked outside my house all night' and you didn't argue with me. You didn't remind me that at this point, the two of us making love is still more of an *if* than a *when*." He looked up at last. His eyes said it all. He wasn't mad.

And he wanted her to stay.

After the uncomfortable moments with Collin at the door and the difficult discussion over dinner, Derek was a little afraid that Amy might decide it was time for her go.

She didn't act like she wanted to go, but he couldn't be sure. Maybe he was reading her all wrong and any minute now she would start edging toward the door.

As she helped him clear the table and load the dishwasher, he considered the various ways to get her to stay.

He knew one surefire method: offer to play video games. She'd always loved them and apparently, she still played them with some dude named Jonas in Boulder.

Yeah, she'd probably mop the floor with him. She used to beat him every time no matter what they played. *Zelda*, *Call of Duty*, *Super Mario Kart*, you name it.

But that was then. Maybe that Jonas guy just wasn't all that good a player. Maybe Amy had lost her touch playing with guys who didn't challenge her—not that he, Derek, was all that much of a challenge to her.

Still, he would like a rematch after all these years, a chance to beat her for once.

He shut the dishwasher door and started it up.

"Well," she said, looking gorgeous and nervous and not sure what would happen next. "I guess maybe I'd better be—"

"Grand Theft Auto V?" he asked.

Worked like a charm. Her grin was slow and full of evil. "It's your funeral."

They went into the great room, kicked off their boots and played.

Just like old times, she whipped his butt.

And then whipped it again.

After two hours of ending up riddled with bullets, buried in a pile of rubble game after game, he dropped his controller onto the coffee table and put up both hands. "I surrender. You win."

She cupped a hand to her ear. "What did you say?"

"You heard me."

"Yeah, but I want you to say it again."

"Amy, you win."

"Yeah!" She dropped her controller next to his, let out a squeal of triumph and did a double fist pump.

"Why don't you go ahead and tell me how you really feel?"

She squealed again and stomped her stocking feet on the floor. "Who's the man?"

"You're the man."

"Say it again! Say it again!" She bounced up and down on the couch, hair flying, eyes squinty, pumping both fists for all she was worth, her red skirt rising temptingly high on her smooth thighs.

Cutest thing he'd ever seen. Strangest girl he'd ever known.

He could not resist her. And why even try? They were together, right? In a nondeclared, open-ended, nobody's-business sort of way. For the next two weeks, at least.

Suddenly, it seemed like a bad idea to waste a single second of the time he might have with her. To hell with waiting. If she was willing, there would be benefits tonight.

He caught her fist in mid-pump. She let out a yelp followed by a goofy giggle as he dragged her close, cupped the back of her head and claimed that delicious mouth of hers.

Another sound escaped her then, breathless and wanting, as she pulled her hand free of his grip and wrapped it around his neck. Her hair was everywhere, glorious and wild around her flushed face, which he cradled between his two palms so he could kiss her some more.

Long, wet kisses. Short, hard kisses. Kisses light as a fleeting touch turning to kisses so deep he drowned in them.

How had he lived all these thirteen endless years without the taste of her mouth, the feel of her silky hair sifting through his fingers, the touch of her velvety skin beneath his hands?

He guided her down on the couch cushions,

kissing her, touching her, smoothing her hair only to spear his fingers in it and mess it up all over again.

She gazed up at him, her eyes full of something he'd never thought he'd see in them again. "Oh, Derek," she whispered, as though his name said it all.

His pulse thudded in his ears and his blood seemed to burn in his veins. "Amy, I…"

"Tell me," she commanded.

"I need to touch you. All of you."

"Yes," she said, so eager. So sure. "Yes. Touch me. All of me. Please."

He wasted no time giving them both what they wanted. Slipping the skinny straps of her little red dress down over her shoulders, he eased the cups of her bra out of his way and buried his face between her soft breasts. She moaned and held him closer.

He needed so much.

All of her.

Naked.

In his hungry arms.

He lifted his head and looked at her, with her dress pulled down, her bra half off, her eyes dazed and dreamy. Her cheeks were a gorgeous shade of pink, her hair in a tangled halo across the nubby cushions of the old couch.

It was the finest sight he'd ever seen.

Something shifted within him. Something opened up wide.

One way or another, they were making it work this time. One way or another they were taking this hesitant, friends-with-benefits second chance all the way to forever.

He didn't know how exactly. Not yet.

But they were older now, and wiser, weren't they? All grown-up and ready to make the big choices and take the important chances, at last.

This time, somehow, they would get it right.

Chapter 7

She pressed a hand to the side of his face and let out a soft little sigh. "Look at us. Is this really happening?"

"You'd better believe it."

She laughed, a giddy, happy sound. "I'm glad. I'm really glad."

He shifted on top of her. "I'm crushing you, aren't I?"

"Derek, I'm fine."

"This couch is too damn small. We're not kids anymore, making love in my pickup out under a tree in the middle of a pasture somewhere."

"Oh, I remember. I used to get bruises from bumping the steering wheel."

"Not anymore. I need to take you to bed, turn on all the lights, look at every inch of you and kiss you all over."

"Yeah." She tugged on his ear and grinned a goofy, blissed-out little grin. "You should do that, all of it. You should do that right now."

He slid off the cushions and bent to gather her up. She raised her arms and wrapped them around his neck. He lifted her high. Kicking a random boot out of his way, he made for the central hall and the shorter hall off it that led to the bedrooms.

His door was wide open. He carried her through and set her down on the rug by the bed. Giggling a little, she readjusted her bra to cover those fine breasts, but left the front of her dress around her waist.

"Stay right there," he commanded. And he left her long enough to get everything right. He shut the curtains and turned on the lights— the standing lamp in the corner, the one on the dresser and the two on the nightstands. He grabbed a few condoms from the nearest nightstand drawer and set them by the clock. Last of all, he turned the covers back to reveal the white sheets.

"I like your house so much," she said. "And this is nice." Her gaze roamed the room, taking it all in. "That's beautiful." She pointed at the tooled leather headboard. "Did you do that yourself?"

"Yeah." He straightened from smoothing the sheet and turned to her. Taking her shoulders, he brought her to face him.

She gazed up at him with shining eyes. "Derek."

"What?"

"Nothing. Just Derek. I always liked saying your name. I still do. The combination of sounds is very satisfying. *D-air-ek*." She chuckled, a soft little whisper of sound. "You think I'm strange. You always did."

"You are one of a kind. Special."

Her bare shoulder lifted in a half shrug. "I'm just plain strange. But thank you for giving it a more positive spin."

He dropped a kiss on that pretty shoulder. "Okay. You're strange—in a special, one-of-a-kind way."

"Derek?"

"Yeah?"

"Kiss my other shoulder."

"Happy to." He pressed his lips to the firm, silky curve, sticking out his tongue and licking the spot for good measure. She gasped just a little. He drank in that sound. "Now." He ran his palm down her arm, caught her fingers and kissed the tips of them. "Take off all your clothes."

"Hmm." She scrunched up her face and pretended to think it over. "I think you should take off my clothes for me."

"And I think that is an excellent idea."

She gazed up at him trustingly as he undid her red belt and tossed it on the bedside chair. Her dress and bra quickly followed.

Now she had only the pair of red socks she'd worn under her boots and little red panties trimmed in pink lace.

"Perfect," he whispered, and bent his head to press his lips to the gorgeous, sweet-smelling curve where her neck met her shoulder. She tasted so good. He couldn't get enough, so he bit her.

"Ouch!" She laughed and slapped at his shoulder. He hauled her against him—and bit her again. "That is going to leave a mark," she complained.

"Tell them we're just friends and it's none of their business."

"You're just asking for it, mister—and why is your shirt still on? That's just not right." She started in on the buttons, her fingers deft and quick. In no time, she was pushing it off his shoulders. He tossed it toward the pile of cloth-ing on the chair as she tugged at the T-shirt he wore underneath.

"Got it." He reached back over his shoulders and pulled it up and off.

"Oh, I do like where this is going," she said with her angel's smile, so completely at ease in her own mostly-naked skin. She'd always been like that with him, even their very first time. Eager and glowing. Adorably awkward. Open. Free. Not what he'd expected of Jack Wain-wright's straight-A student, virgin daughter.

She spread her hands on his belly and slowly glided them upward. "I do believe this is an eight-pack you've got going on here."

"Hard work and clean living will do that to a man." Would he ever get enough of the feel of her touch?

Not a chance.

Those caressing hands glided up and over his shoulders. They met at his nape and kept going, her fingers sliding into his hair, mas-saging his scalp.

He had a feeling of stark unreality. That this was too perfect a moment to be true. "Am I dreaming?"

"If you are," she said low and achingly

sweet, "so am I. We're dreaming this together and all I want is for us never to wake up."

He clasped her bare waist. "You're real."

"Oh, yes." She let her head drop back and closed her eyes. The feathery ends of her hair brushed his hands.

He slid his palms up over the cage of her ribs, bringing them around between them to cup both breasts, one in either hand. They were plump and so pretty, a little fuller than he remembered. She still had that tiny, heart-shaped mole over her left nipple.

No way he could resist bending to kiss that.

And then, well, he just went on kissing her, pressing his lips to the slope of her breast and then the beautiful swell on the underside. She let out a sweet, pleasured cry and pulled him closer, guiding him to where she wanted him.

His mouth closed on her tight nipple as her head fell back. She gave a low moan when he drew on her, using his teeth, circling with his tongue.

"Yes. Oh, please," she whispered as he moved to the other breast.

He still wore his jeans and his erection pressed almost painfully against his zipper, pulling even tighter as he went to his knees. Slowly, taking his time about it, he sank toward the rug, kissing his way between the delicate swells of her rib cage, down the velvety flesh of her belly. He paused to dip his tongue in her navel, bringing a sweet gasp from her.

Her lower belly was silky-smooth, with just that little bit of tempting roundness he remembered so well. He kissed the spot, his mind wandering briefly to the tiny, unformed baby that might have been sleeping there, once, long ago.

But that was the past.

Foolish to dwell on it.

Better to give himself up to right now, to the wonderful, womanly feel of her against his mouth, under his hands.

He scraped his teeth along her hip bones, and then, bringing low moans from her, he took her panties in either hand and eased them down.

"Derek, oh, yes. That!" she cried, as he pressed his lips to the neatly trimmed strip of dark hair that led to the female heart of her. And then she sighed, "Oh, exactly *that*..."

And she didn't stop there. She added more tender, hungry encouragements as her fingers tunneled through his hair. She watched as he played her, as he drank in her sweetness, worked her with his tongue, using his fingers, too, both to stroke her and to hold her in place for his eager kiss.

When she broke wide open, he just went on kissing her, riding it out with her. He loved the sounds she made, the frantic, harsh rhythm of each ragged breath, the way her fingers dug into his scalp, yanking him closer as she pressed her core tighter to his never-ending kiss.

"Derek," she whispered. "Oh, Derek..." And she framed his face in her shaking hands and urged him to look up at her. For one glorious moment, he took in the sight of her, eyes dazed and shining, mouth softly parted, her hair on her shoulders, a few long curls veiling her pretty breasts.

"You are so beautiful, Amy."

With a yearning little cry, she urged him up.

He swept to his feet and she went on tiptoe to kiss him, laughing a little when she stumbled on her panties. They were tangled around one of her ankles. He dropped to the rug again, lifted her foot and removed both her sock and the twisted-up bit of satin and lace. She braced a hand on his shoulder as he slipped off her other sock.

Then she pulled him up again and got after the task of unhooking his belt and unzipping his jeans.

"Lie down." Hands spread on his chest, she pressed gently but insistently, until he let himself fall back across the mattress. It took her only a moment to pull off his jeans and get rid of his socks.

"Come here." He caught her hand and pulled her down next to him.

She landed at his side with a happy sigh, tucking her head into the crook of his shoulder, nuzzling his throat as her naughty hand strayed downward. When she touched him, he almost unraveled right there, with her hand barely brushing him. Even with his boxer briefs in the way, her touch thrilled and burned.

"Such a long time," she said softly, trailing her fingers back up his body to cradle his cheek.

"It's felt like forever," he agreed. He'd been so lonely without her, so empty inside. Should he admit that?

No.

A man had to have a little pride, after all.

"Forget everything," she whispered, her warm breath in his ear, the brush of her plump lower lip against his earlobe. "Let the world disappear. We'll stay here in bed and we'll never leave."

"I wish." But he couldn't quite make that promise. "Life…interrupts."

"Shh." She caught his earlobe between her teeth and gave it a tug. "For now, for tonight, pretend that it's possible. You and me, together in this comfy bed for all eternity."

As a fantasy, it rang all his bells. "Yes, Miss Wainwright."

She guided him to face her with the gentle pressure of her palm against his cheek. "That's more like it." Their lips met, proving all over again that there was nothing in the wide world as good as her kiss.

He tasted her deeply, letting himself believe that he would never have to let her go, that the promise he'd made to himself—the two of them, working it out, getting it right this time—was bound to come true.

And when she took her lips from his to move down his body, he tried to hold her there, face-to-face with him, tried to kiss her some more. But she had other plans.

They were excellent plans, really. She got rid of his boxer briefs and took him in her hand.

And in her mouth.

It was so good. Too good.

He looked down his body at her head bobbing up and down on him, her hair caressing his belly, spilling like silk over his thighs. Bliss.

And if he didn't put a stop to this soon, he would lose it. He didn't want that. Not for their first time in all these years and years. For their first time, he needed to be joined with her, needed to feel her go over the edge again before his finish claimed him.

She made a sharp sound of disapproval as he took her under the arms and pulled her back up so they were face-to-face. Eyes low and lazy, mouth in a pout, she demanded, "What? I was busy."

"Too busy."

A slow grin tipped the corners of her red, swollen lips as she reached down and wrapped her hand around him all over again.

"Be good," he commanded.

She gave a snorty little laugh. "Oh, I am. You know I am. I am very, very, very good."

He felt for a condom, found it and reached down to capture that naughty hand of hers. "Here." He pressed the condom into her palm and folded her fingers over it.

"Well, all right, then." She brushed a kiss to his jaw. "Since you put it that way…" She got rid of the pouch and rolled the condom down over him, careful not to pinch or poke it, smoothing it nice and tight at the base.

Once that was accomplished, she met his

eyes. "I've got an IUD," she said solemnly. "Double protection. We should be safe."

Safe.

Not really.

True, with a condom *and* an IUD, they had just about zero possibility of making a baby.

But there were so many other ways this was not safe—not safe at all. She'd cut his heart to pieces once. And this, now?

Talk about playing with fire.

So what? Some second chances a man just couldn't pass up. No matter how it all shook out in the end, he was in this with her now. All the way.

He had one arm around her and he used it to pull her closer, bringing his mouth a breath's distance from hers. "I'm just glad. You can't know how glad I am to be here with you like this."

She whispered his name again and then they were kissing, a deep and never-ending kiss. He rolled her under him and eased his thigh between her legs. She opened for him eagerly, lifting her body toward him as he sank into her.

Bracing on his hands, he lifted away enough to gaze down at her. She moaned in protest at the broken kiss. "Come back here."

In response, he pressed in deeper, but he

didn't give her the kiss she demanded. He remained braced above her. "Amy."

She knew what he wanted. She opened her eyes.

"Real," he said on a harsh breath, staring down into her heavy-lidded eyes. Her pupils had blown wide with pleasure. They looked as dark as the middle of the night. Dark and deep and shining, promising all the things he'd stopped daring to dream of.

He wanted it all with her, wanted so much to believe that they could make it work together, at last.

But whatever happened in the end, right now, she was with him, her body soft and welcoming beneath him.

"Real," she agreed, surging against him.

The rest was a tangle of limbs and breath and seeking hands. He didn't know the things he said. She answered him in kind, pleading words, tender, too—and sometimes words of hot demand. They didn't really matter, the meaning in the words, the wildly whispered promises.

Only *she* mattered, her softness and her urgent sighs, her skin to his skin, her body holding him, owning him, taking him deep. Her scent like honey and citrus and roses and musk.

He held out against his climax, somehow, waiting for her, moving in her slowly, until she caught her ride to the finish, rocking faster when she needed a swifter, harder rhythm.

When she cried out, he stilled in her, pressing deep as her body pulsed so perfectly around him. Braced up on his hands again, he looked down at her. He watched her slow glide from the crest to afterglow.

Only then did he move again, propelling her into another rise.

That time, he went with her, to the top of the world and over. They rose together.

And together, they fell.

"I should go," she whispered.

He settled the covers more snugly around her. "It's two in the morning. Give it up. Spend the night."

"But Eva will—"

"Don't you even start worrying about Eva." He brushed the hair back from her forehead and dropped a kiss there. "She knows where you are and she's happy that you're here."

"Hmm," she said, which told him exactly nothing.

"Hmm, what?" He kissed her temple. She

had so many good places for him to put his mouth.

She snuggled in closer. "Hmm, I think you might be right."

"You *know* I'm right." He kissed the side of her nose. "Now, go to sleep."

She yawned. "Do you provide breakfast?"

"Why? You hungry now?"

"No. I just wondered. I mean, you said it yourself. You used to be a guy who didn't stick around for breakfast."

"Used to be. Which means those days are over. Plus, if I don't stick around for breakfast, where would I go? This is my house."

She laughed. "Now you're confusing me."

"Let me make it crystal clear." He pressed his lips to hers. "Stay."

In the morning, Amy woke to the inviting smells of fresh coffee and frying bacon. The clock on the nightstand said it was a little after seven.

She shoved back the covers and pulled on her panties. Too bad her red dress, tossed in a wad across the bedside chair, was nothing but a bunch of wrinkles.

In the bathroom, she used the toilet and rinsed last night's mascara from under her eyes. There was toothpaste in the drawer by the sink. She used her finger as a toothbrush.

On the hook behind the door, she found a dark blue robe. It smelled like Derek's piney aftershave and was about three sizes too big.

Still. It was better than her wrinkled dress.

Derek, shirtless and barefoot in jeans that rode low on his narrow hips, was stirring scrambled eggs at the stove when she entered the kitchen from the central hallway. She had a few seconds to admire the gorgeous, hard curve of his shoulder and the sculpted muscles of his chest and belly before he glanced over and saw her.

His leaf-green gaze ran over her, stirring up sparks, hot little flares of sensation, reminders of all they'd done the night before. "You found my robe. It looks good on you."

She flapped the ends of the too-big arms at him. "Perfect fit." She shook her head. "Maybe I should have thought this through more carefully, though. I've got nothing but last night's rumpled red dress to wear back to Sunshine Farm. Talk about your classic walk of shame."

He turned off the fire under the eggs. "We'll figure something out." And then he was coming for her, his bare feet silent on the wide planks of the kitchen floor. He caught one of the sleeves she'd flapped at him and pulled her close. "Let's try this again. Say 'Good morning.'"

"Good morning." She gazed up at him, her heart aching in the best kind of way. To be here in his house, on a sunny Saturday morning, bacon and eggs and coffee waiting, his big hand brushing slow and lazy up and down her arm, thrilling her even through the thick terry cloth of his robe, his eyes for her alone. It was her own most impossible fantasy come true.

"Say, 'I had an amazing time last night, Derek. I can't wait to do it again.'"

"Yeah," she answered, thinking of his kisses, of how right it felt to be with him again, at last, in the most intimate way. "That's true. I can't wait."

He clasped the arm that he'd been stroking and pulled her in closer. His lips covered hers in a slow, perfect kiss. When he lifted his head, he turned for the stove again.

She stared after him, bemused. *Happy*, she thought. *Right in this moment, I'm as happy as I've ever been.*

"You hungry?" He picked up the pan full of eggs.

"Very." She glanced toward the breakfast nook. He'd already set the table.

"Pour yourself some coffee and let's eat."

* * *

Her phone, left on the central island the night before, rang as she was loading the dishwasher. Derek set down the plate of leftover bacon and got it for her.

It was still bleating out a ringtone when he handed it over. She looked at the display. "It's my mom." Stepping to the end of the counter, she put the phone back down and returned to her task. Derek hadn't moved. She probably should say something. "She'll leave a message."

"You don't want to talk to her." It wasn't a question. His gaze was locked on her face, reading her much too easily, the way he always had.

She opened the dishwasher, stuck in a plate and straightened. "All these years and they never told me that my dad went after you to convince you to call it off with me. I don't want to talk to either of them now. Not till I'm ready to brace them with the fact that I do not appreciate them keeping the truth from me—and don't even try to tell me that she might not know. Maybe she doesn't know. That's not the point. If I talk to her, I'm bringing it up and I'm not ready to get into it with either of them yet." As she grabbed the other plate, her phone buzzed from the end of the counter. She had a voice mail.

Derek stepped up close, gently took the plate from her and set it back in the sink. "Think about it. It wasn't a bad thing he did. He loved you and he wanted to make sure you had the best kind of start in life."

"He should have told me what he did—if not that very day, then later. He's had *years* to cop to it. And he's never said a word." She turned and picked up the plate again.

That time, he didn't stop her.

When they finished cleaning up the kitchen, he led her to the bedroom, where he found a Zac Brown Band T-shirt and an old pair of jeans for her. "The shirt's too big and you'll need to roll up the jeans," he warned as he handed them over.

"They'll be great, thanks."

He bent enough to brush a kiss across her lips. "I've got to meet up with Eli and a couple of my cousins in an hour. We need to move some cattle and burn out a ditch or two."

"Darn. I was kind of picturing us spending the whole day without a stitch on."

He rubbed the back of his neck, his expression rueful, the beautiful muscles of his arm flexing so temptingly as he moved. "Sometimes there's no upside to ranch life."

She went on tiptoe and kissed him again. "Tonight, then?"

He hooked his arm around her waist and brought her up hard and close. "Yes." The kiss he gave her then curled her toes and practically set her hair on fire. When he finally let her go, he asked, "How are we doing on the party supplies?"

"We've got everything we need, so at least the shopping part's done. But we still have signs to make and decorations and such to pull together before the big push next Saturday. We're talking several hours of crafting."

"Crafting." He faked a scared expression, all wide eyes and hanging mouth. "Now, there's a word to strike terror in the hearts of men everywhere."

"If you're not going to help me, I'll have to get Eva to pitch in."

It took him a moment to realize she meant that as a threat. "Wait. I get it. She's the bride and having the bride pitch in on the bachelor party would be wrong. Am I right?"

She reached up and patted his warm, beard-scruffy cheek. "Give that man a gold star. So I was thinking that a couple of hours an evening should do it."

He had that look men get when women sign

them up for things they're just going to have to endure. "How many evenings?"

"Well, how about we start with tonight and see how it goes? I would bring the stuff we need and we can put it together here, if that works for you."

"Two hours of crafting? Here? Tonight?"

"I'll bring takeout," she coaxed.

He guided a swatch of her hair behind her ear and then skated the back of his finger down the bridge of her nose. "I've got some steaks. We're good for tonight."

"Steaks would be excellent."

He took her hand, pressed a key into her palm and folded her fingers over it. "Now you can come on in whether I'm here or not."

Was a key too much, too soon? "I don't know if I feel comfortable taking—"

He stopped her with a finger to her lips. "Between the saddlery and the ranch, I've always got something going on. If you get here before me one of these nights, I don't want you having to wait on the porch."

It was thoughtful of him, really. And to keep arguing would just be making a big deal of it. "Okay. Um, thanks, then. What time works for you tonight?"

"That's the thing. I could be back here at two or three—or it could be later."

"Six?" she suggested.

"That'll work for sure. And after the steaks and the crafting, you'll stay over?"

She kissed him again. "I thought you'd never ask."

Eva was lying in wait for her at Sunshine Farm. "Nice T-shirt. I never made you for a Zac Brown fan."

"I love the Zac Brown Band. 'Chicken Fried' is my favorite song—and aren't you supposed to be at Daisy's?" Eva worked at Daisy's Donuts, sometimes serving customers, but mostly producing an endless array of totally amazing baked goods.

"I've been cutting back my hours lately, what with the wedding and everything. Today, I'm off." She grabbed Amy's arm. "Come in the kitchen. We need to talk."

Amy tried to hang back. "I need to put my wrinkled dress away. And a shower would be so nice."

But Eva just took the red dress from her, plunked it on the entry table and kept on pulling her toward the other room. "This won't take long." About two seconds later, Eva had her sitting at the table with a full mug of coffee. "Jumbo caramel-banana-nut muffin?" She set a plateful of them on the table.

The nutty, caramel-banana scent was amazing. Amy took one. Who could resist? "Oh, Eva." She moaned in pleasure at the first bite. "They're still warm."

"Enjoy." Eva gave her a dessert plate and a fork, pulled out the chair beside her and plunked down into it. "And tell me *everything*."

Amy sipped coffee and gobbled her muffin and explained the basics. "Derek and I are going to be spending some time together, that's all. Just for while I'm here. I mean, we have the party to plan and—"

Eva let out a musical trill of laughter. "Oh. Right. You spent all last night together working on the bachelor party. You must be exhausted."

Amy groaned. "Fine. We've kind of…reconnected."

Eva tipped her head to the side with a puzzled frown. "Reconnected. That sounds a little clinical, don't you think?"

"You don't like *reconnected*?"

"No, I do not."

"Well, all right, then. What should I call it?"

"Oh, let's see. How about *fated forever lovers reunited at last*?"

"Eva Rose, you are a hopeless romantic."

"And proud of it, too. Tell me more about this 'reconnecting' you've been doing."

"Well, I mean, we're going to see where it takes us. Because we still get along."

Eva scrunched up her nose as though something smelled bad. "You 'get along'?"

"Yes, we do." Amy sipped her coffee and ate more of the delicious muffin.

"Ugh." Eva threw up both hands and plopped them back into her lap with a loud slapping sound. "That's it? That's all you're going to tell me?"

"Eva, I love you. But this is private, you know?"

"Private is fine," argued Eva. "I won't tell a soul. Come on. Please. You have to give me *something*. I'm your friend forever and I'm dying to know what's going on."

Amy relented—marginally, anyway. She did trust Eva and she hated disappointing her. "Well, I'm going back to his place for dinner tonight."

Eva's frown vanished. "Okay, I love the sound of that."

"We'll spend a couple of hours putting props and decorations together for the party. We'll be doing that pretty much every night this week—at least, until we finish the job."

"And of course, you'll be staying over at Derek's place afterward. I mean, it's just a bad idea for you to drive all the way back here when you're all worn out from making party decorations."

Amy blotted up delicious muffin crumbs with her fork and ate them. "Yes. That's right. I'll be staying over at his place. At least for tonight."

Eva put her hand on Amy's arm and gave it a squeeze. "I'm so grateful the two of you are working so hard on the party. It's going to be such fun, I just know it." She giggled.

Amy couldn't help it. She giggled right along with her. "I do, um, like him, Eva. I still do like him a lot."

"He's a good man," said Eva.

"He is, yes."

"I'm so glad you're giving it another chance with him."

Amy drew back a little. Eva would keep her confidence, absolutely. But still, she'd made such a big deal with Derek about keeping things just between the two of them. "Friends, Eva. Derek and I are friends."

"Of course, you are," agreed Eva. "And friends have sleepovers, now don't they? I'm seeing a lot of sleepovers at Derek's in your future and I am very, very happy about that."

Chapter 8

Derek was waiting on his front porch when Amy arrived that evening.

He ran down the steps and pulled open her door. "I thought you'd never get here." His hair was still damp from a shower, his cheeks freshly shaven. He was and always had been the best-looking guy she'd ever known.

She reminded him, "We said six. I'm right on time."

He didn't argue, just grabbed her hand and pulled her out from behind the wheel. Right there by the car, he wrapped his arms around her and kissed her until her head spun, after which he bent to slide one arm under her legs and scoop her up against his chest.

She let out a laughing cry. "Derek!"

"Let's go inside."

Still laughing, she hooked one arm around his neck and pointed through the back window of her Audi. "I've got my overnight case and all the party stuff we need to bring in."

"Later for that." And he kissed her again— kissed her and went on kissing her as he carried her up the steps and into the house. He kicked the door shut with his boot and took her straight to his bedroom, where they remained for the next two hours.

At a little after eight, they put their clothes back on and went out to unload the car. They brought everything in and then got dinner ready.

It was after nine when they finally started working on the signs for the casino and the scavenger hunt. When those were done, they wrapped party-favor prizes. Midnight had come and gone by the time they carted their finished work into Derek's spare room, where it would remain until the day of the party.

"Tomorrow, we'll figure out all the questions for The Nearly Newlywed Game," she said as they left the room. "We need twenty for Eva about Luke and twenty for him about her." He pulled the door shut behind them and took her hand. "They need to be funny questions, kind of hard, but not *too* hard…" He wrapped their joined hands behind his back, which brought her right up tight against him, and gave new meaning to the word *hard*. All the breath left her body and a thousand fluttery creatures took flight in her belly.

"No more party talk tonight," he growled as he nuzzled her ear.

"Poor baby." She went on tiptoe to feather a line of kisses down the side of his throat. "You must be exhausted."

"Yeah. We should go to bed."

She had zero objections to that suggestion. He kept a firm grip on her hand as he turned for the open door to the master suite.

Once inside, he started peeling off her clothes.

"You know, Derek. Suddenly, you don't seem the least bit tired."

And then he kissed her and she forgot everything but the glory of his touch.

Sunday morning after breakfast, they came up with The Nearly Newlywed Game questions for Eva and Luke.

As they made sandwiches for lunch, Amy got a text from Eva. "She wants us to come to dinner at the farm tonight. Six o'clock."

"I'm in."

Amy texted back that they would be there and returned to slicing tomatoes for turkey-on-rye.

But Derek took the knife from her and turned her to face him. "I want every minute I can have with you."

She wasn't sure what he was getting at. "Didn't we already agree to that?"

"We did, but tonight when it's time to come home and whoever else Eva invited notices you're going with me, don't chicken out on me and suddenly decide you might as well just stay at Luke and Eva's. I want you with me."

Her heart kind of melted. "No, I won't back out. When it's time to go, I'll follow you home."

He brushed his warm lips against hers. "That's what I needed to hear."

The evening was a lot of fun. It was just the four of them and Bailey, who was thoroughly charming when he chose to be. They had Eva's amazing roast chicken with herbed potatoes and a chocolate trifle for dessert.

Eva and Luke were so cute, exchanging random quick kisses, holding hands every chance they got, sitting extra close to each other on the couch, two people truly together and deeply in love.

Watching them, Amy felt just a little bit wistful. To be in love like that, to be half of a private world inhabited by two—she and Derek had been like that once. No other guy had ever made her feel the way he had, that she was the only one he'd ever wanted, the only one for him.

Which was why she needed to be careful with him, not let herself get too carried away. Now and then, she would catch herself about to reach out and touch him, wanting to lean close and whisper something tender in his ear.

But she didn't. Throughout the evening, she and Derek kept to their agreement. They played it friends-only, with zero PDAs.

Amy had brought the two lists of Nearly Newlywed Game questions. She gave one to Luke and one to Eva. "We'll need these back tomorrow, if possible, so we can get going on making a proper display for this game. There will be two sets of boards, one set without the answers, so everyone can read your questions and guess the answers, then another set to put out when we announce the winners. Those will have your answers on them. I'm putting you two on the honor system," she warned. "I want your word you won't share your questions with each other or cheat on the answers."

"Don't be scared, you two," Derek advised with a grin. "It's just that Amy takes her party planning seriously."

As if there was anything wrong with that. "Yes, I do," she said, "and I'm proud of it, too."

Eva put up a hand like a witness swearing an oath. "I do solemnly promise to answer all my questions myself and not to help Luke with his no matter how hard he begs me."

"Excellent." Amy turned her gaze on Eva's fiancé. "Luke?"

He put up *both* hands. "Okay, okay. I promise, too."

Bailey grumbled, "I gotta say it. Amy, when it comes to this party, you're definitely scaring *me*."

She pinned Luke's brother with a severe frown. "Don't you start in, Bailey Stockton. Party planning is a tough job and you are one of the groomsmen, which means you really ought to be helping Derek and me pull this thing together."

Bailey, who'd taken the leftover seat at one

end of the sofa, bent at the waist and thunked his head against the coffee table. "Anything but that."

Everybody laughed as Eva got up to get the coffeepot in case anyone wanted one more cup.

When it was time to go, Amy slipped away to run up to her room and grab a change of clothes for tomorrow. She and Derek thanked Eva for the great meal and headed for the door.

"Good night, Luke," Amy said. "Bailey…" She turned to give Bailey a smile.

He glanced from her to Derek and back again. He didn't say anything, but he didn't have to. The speculative look on his face said it all.

Which was fine.

To be expected.

People were going to notice that they were together. And they'd agreed on how to deal with that: no PDAs and continued denial till after the wedding.

And then?

She'd been thinking about that. A lot. And she really did hope that after the wedding they could talk honestly about the future, about ways that maybe they might really try again.

But as for now, Amy did love a good plan

and so far, this one seemed to be working just great.

She was having the time of her life with her secret ex-husband and every hour that passed had her feeling more certain that this time, they would get it right.

It was going so well.

What could possibly go wrong?

Monday morning, Derek woke next to Amy.

He rolled over and gathered her close, spoon fashion. "Derek…" He could hear her sleepy smile in her voice. She snuggled right in with a happy little sigh and drifted back to sleep.

In a few minutes, he had to get up. It was his turn to open at the saddlery and he needed to be there by eight.

But a few minutes went by and a few more after that, and he lay there in bed with Amy in his arms, her hair a shining, red-brown tangle across the white pillow, her breathing shallow and slow.

What was it about her? He couldn't really put his finger on it. She was bossy, strong-minded and really smart. Maybe too smart for a small-town cowboy like him. She made him laugh. She made him think—about what he wanted and how to get it.

She made everything better, somehow.

No other girl had ever compared.

He was beginning to face the truth that if he didn't have Amy, well, he probably wouldn't have anyone. Not in the way that really mattered, the forever way, the way Collin had Willa, the way Luke had Eva.

All these years, he'd been telling himself he was slowly getting over her, that at some point, it would happen. He'd look in the bathroom mirror one morning and see a man who didn't love Amy Wainwright anymore.

But now, here she was, back in town. And miracle of miracles, back in his bed.

And all he could think about was how he was going to keep her here, his own bossy little angel, sleeping beside him for the rest of their lives.

Collin's crew cab was already parked in front of the saddlery when Derek got there at 8:10.

"You're early," Derek said when he found his partner sitting at the table in the break room, a full mug of coffee in front of him.

Collin pointed at the chair across from him. "I was hoping we might have a chance to talk before the kid comes in."

Derek brewed himself a cup, though he'd already had two back at the house. He was stalling, putting off the inevitable just a little bit longer.

But it only took so long to brew a pod of coffee. He set the mug on the table and dropped into the chair. "Okay. Got a problem with my work or something?"

Collin barked out a dry laugh. "You wish." He aimed a brooding look at his full cup, but didn't pick it up. "So. Amy Wainwright?"

"Saying her name with a question mark after it doesn't count as an actual question, Collin."

"She's a nice girl. I always liked her. I got nothing against her."

"Yeah? So, then what's this about?"

Collin tipped his head thoughtfully—and then went on as though Derek hadn't spoken. "Her father was kind of a douche nozzle, though. Snotty rich guy. Had to get back to the land, or some such, but always kept himself above the rest of us."

"Jack Wainwright wasn't so bad."

Collin scoffed, "Really? You're going to defend him?"

Derek rubbed the bridge of his nose between his thumb and forefinger. "Whatever it is you're trying to say here, you need to just come out with it."

Collin did sip his coffee then. "We never talked about that night of the bonfire, the night you got wasted and told me all your secrets." Collin stared across the table at him, dark gaze unwavering. "Don't worry. I never said a word to anyone about any of it and I damn well never will."

Derek's gut kind of felt like a big boot had kicked it. "I always wondered how much I told you."

"You said that you and Amy thought she was pregnant and so you'd gotten married, but then it turned out she wasn't pregnant. You said that the original plan was for Amy to go off to college and since there was no baby after all, it was back to the plan. She was moving to Colorado to go to school and you expected you'd be getting divorce papers in the mail. You said that you loved her and you always would, but you hated her, too, for walking out on you."

Derek swore. "I had no right to say that she walked out on me. I told her to go."

"But you didn't think she'd really leave you, did you? You thought she'd fight to keep your marriage together."

"I'll say it again. I told her to go."

"You were wrecked over her. That girl ruined you. I didn't understand then, how deep she'd cut you. But now I have Willa. If Willa ever did something like that to me, I don't rightly know if I would ever recover." Collin fell silent. He stared into the middle distance.

Derek almost dared to hope his friend had said all he meant to say.

No such luck.

"Guys like you and me, we go from girl to girl. And people judge us. They think we haven't got deep feelings. But could be it's the opposite. Maybe our feelings run too damn deep and if we ever give in and give a woman everything, and she turns around and leaves us…" Collin let that thought finish itself. He asked, "You sure you want to go tempting fate all over again?" Derek just looked at him. Collin didn't need an answer anyway. He already understood. "I know. I do. She's the one for you and at this point, while it's good between you, before it gets down to where the rubber hits the road, you can't walk away. But you need to remember how good you are at leaving. You need to remind yourself what a natural talent you have for letting go. It's what you know how to do. Don't let your bad habits rule you. Don't fold before the game's even over.

Step up and just say it. This time, when you're ready to run, tell the woman straight out that you love her and you want her to stay."

After Derek left for the saddlery that morning, Amy went back to Sunshine Farm. She had work to catch up on and spent most of the day at her computer.

When she went downstairs to make a sandwich at noon, Eva joined her in the kitchen.

"Here are both your questionnaires." Eva handed them over. "They're all filled out and ready to go—and don't give me that look. Luke gave me his to give to you, but I have not even glanced at it."

"Good." Amy took them.

Eva let out a wry little laugh. "Bailey may have had a point last night. The good Lord have mercy on anyone who messes with your plans."

"Nothing wrong with careful planning. Just watch. This party is going to be amazing."

"I know it will be—and I keep forgetting to tell you that Friday night, after you left the Ace, Viv asked me if you needed help with anything."

"Not a thing. We're so on it. And I have kept in touch with her. Just this morning, I

texted her a suggested playlist for the band."
In her back pocket, Amy's phone rang. It was
the ringtone she'd assigned to her dad and she
ignored it, letting it ring until it stopped. She
answered Eva's questioning glance with, "It's
my dad. I'll call him back later. Right now, I
need lunch."

"How about a roast chicken sandwich with
mayo, walnuts and cranberry sauce?"

"I thought you'd never ask."

That evening after a beautiful hour in bed
together, Derek said that he and Collin had
talked. "Turns out, I did tell him pretty much
everything that night I got so drunk." He put
a finger under her chin and tipped her face up
so she was looking at him. "I'm sorry I broke
my promise not to tell anyone."

She lifted up higher—enough to press a reassuring kiss on those fine lips of his. "Well,
when I left, I kind of gave up my right to ask
for your silence. You were on your own and
I'm really not upset that you told him. I think
it was good that you had someone to talk to.
And Collin clearly knows how to keep a confidence. I mean, *you* didn't even know he knew."

He chuckled, a rueful sound. "True."

"Did he…warn you off me?" Should she

even ask him that? Probably not. But she really wanted to know.

Derek's silence lasted just a moment too long. "He was just being a friend, you know? Showing his support."

She got the message. Derek had said all he wanted to say. Pushing him to reveal more wouldn't be right. She left it at that, tucking her head in under his chin as he pulled the covers up closer around them.

Amy spent that night and the next and the next after that at Derek's.

Their nobody's-business, one-day-at-a-time relationship was working out so well. She spent four or five hours a day at Sunshine Farm, being with Eva and keeping on top of her work with Hurdly and Main.

In the early evening, she would meet Derek at his house. They would have dinner and put in some work on the party, after which they would watch a movie or play video games— sometimes not finishing either and having glorious sex instead. Eventually, they would go to bed, where yet more gloriousness ensued.

Every moment with him was better than the moment before and she never wanted it to end.

Which they would have to talk about.

Eventually.

But at this point, they were living firmly in the now and she wouldn't have it any other way.

Wednesday night, they finished the party prep. There was literally nothing more to do until setup on Saturday.

Thursday, they met at his place at two in the afternoon. They tacked up a couple of horses and rode out across Circle D land to a private spot on Rust Creek, a bend in the stream where the water ran slow and deep.

They hobbled the horses. And in the shade of a river birch, they spread a blanket and stripped down to their birthday suits. The water was cold and they laughed and splashed each other, chasing each other back and forth across the slow-moving stream. He dunked her twice and she managed to shove him under once, just to prove that she could.

They ended up on the blanket, making love in the dappled shade of the tree. Afterward, they put their clothes back on and lay side by side, holding hands, staring up through the wind-ruffled cottonwood leaves at the wide blue sky.

She had so much to tell him, all the secrets of her heart, the longing in her soul. She needed him to know how much she had missed him all the years they'd been apart, needed to confess that she couldn't help dreaming of a possible future with him.

Too bad she had no idea how to even start saying all that she yearned to say.

She rolled her head toward him. He was already watching her. She drank in the sight of him, his square, beard-scruffy jaw, his eyes, green as shamrocks right now, the perfect, sexy dent in the center of his chin. "I never want to leave you. I want to stay here forever, Derek, just you and me."

He gave her that smile, the one that made her heart stop and her belly hollow out. "Right here under this tree?"

Should she go for it, go all the way right here and now? Was it too early?

How did people do this? Start over. Really begin. She hardly knew how. She'd done it so badly the last time. She hadn't been brave enough.

Hadn't been true enough.

And now she had another chance—or at least, she hoped that was what this might be. She didn't want to blow it. She didn't want to push too fast.

Or miss the moment when it was finally upon her.

Would she mess it up this time, too, and lose him all over again?

Her heart knocked against her rib cage and her pulse raced.

He used the hand that wasn't holding hers, reaching across his broad chest to brush a slow, wonderfully rough finger along the line of her jaw. "You all right?"

Not yet! screeched a terrified voice in her head. *Don't say anything yet! Get a grip. It's way too soon. You'll ruin everything.*

"Yeah." Her heart rate slowed and she dared to breathe again as she chose the easy way out. "I was thinking we could make a little shelter here, a hut of sticks and pine branches."

He lifted their joined hands and pressed his lips to her knuckles, one by one. Gladness filled her so full, she felt she might burst apart. She said, "It could get mighty cold when winter comes."

"Well then, we'd have to get under the blanket and hold each other really tight." To demonstrate, he rolled toward her, reaching for her, gathering her close, sheltering her in the strength of his arms.

I love you, Derek. I always have. You are

the only man for me. It sounded so good inside her head. So good and so true.

And she *would* say it. Just not now, not so soon.

Later. When the time was right.

Friday, Eva's sisters were due to arrive: Delphine, her husband, Harrison, and their three boys from Billings; and Calla, her husband, Patrick, and their two kids from Thunder Canyon.

Amy planned to spend the day at the Armstrong house in town. It would be so good, to get some quality time not only with Delphine and Calla and their families, but also with Marion and Ray Armstrong, who'd been like a second mother and father to her while she was growing up.

She saw Derek off at his house early that morning when he went out to cut alfalfa with Eli and his cousins, and she promised to meet him back there after the big family dinner at Ray and Marion's.

"It might be late," she warned him. "Delphine and Calla and I have a lot of catching up to do."

"I don't care if it's the middle of the night when they finally let you out of there. We agreed every night for as long as you're here, remember?"

Had they agreed on that? She wasn't really sure. But whether they had or they hadn't, she wanted every night she could get with him. "Well, all right then. I'll be here. Leave the porch light on."

He kissed her, a long, deep one. And then she stood in the yard, waving and grinning like a lovestruck fool as he started up his truck and headed off down the dirt ranch road toward the main house and the barn.

Eva was already at the two-story Armstrong family home in town when Amy arrived at nine. Delphine and Calla and their families had set out long before dawn. Of the two older sisters, Delphine got there first at a little after eleven. Calla and her crew arrived just before noon.

They all shared lunch out in the backyard. It was just like old times, except with even more of them, now that Calla's and Delphine's husbands and active youngsters had been added to the mix. Amy could almost grow wistful with her friends' children all around. At ten years old, Calla's daughter, Fiona, was becoming such a young lady. And Delphine's oldest,

Tommy, was already nine. Amy marveled at how fast they were all growing up.

And she couldn't help feeling a little bit sad. If she and Derek had stayed together, they would have recently celebrated thirteen years of marriage. Their might-have-been baby would be twelve now, the oldest of the children in the Armstrong backyard.

Luke showed up at a little after five. He came in the door and Eva ran to greet him. Amy felt a sharp, painful tug on her heartstrings that Derek couldn't somehow be there, too. Eva and her sisters had all found love. Amy was the only single adult in the bunch today. They all looked so happy, with their lives, their loves, their families.

What would they say if they knew she'd been married before any of them?

Married and divorced before she was even nineteen.

Nobody was going to congratulate her for that.

As they gathered around the big dining room table to sit down for dinner, there was a knock at the door.

Luke said, "That's Derek. I'll get it."

Amy's heart leapt—and she didn't m͟ sly grin that Eva tried to hide.

Yep. No doubt about it. Her lifelong BFF was matchmaking like crazy.

And at this point, all Amy felt about that was love and gratitude.

When he returned to the room, Luke said, "You all remember Derek, my best man."

Derek's hair was still damp from his shower and he looked so hot and handsome in a green-and-black plaid snap-front shirt and dress jeans.

Delphine and Calla both jumped up to give him a quick hug of greeting. Introductions were made to the husbands and kids—reintroductions really. Derek, it turned out, had met both Delphine's and Calla's husbands over the years and more than one of the kids.

"Have a seat, everyone," said Marion.

Eva piped up with, "Derek, there's a free chair next to Amy."

Derek came right over, pulled out Amy's chair for her and then sat down beside her. She leaned toward the man who owned her nights—at least until the wedding—and greeted him teasingly, "Derek. So nice to see you again."

"Yeah." His gaze held hers and a delicious little shiver skittered down her spine and tickled the backs of her knees. "We need to get to-ether more often."

She didn't look away. "I think that can be arranged. How come you didn't tell me you were coming for dinner?"

"Because I didn't know I was coming until Luke called this afternoon and invited me."

Amy slid another glance at Eva, who was still watching them, still trying to hide her self-satisfied grin. "Did you have to skip Friday happy hour at the Ace?" Amy teased the man beside her.

"To tell you the truth, I wasn't planning on dropping by there anyway. Hanging out at the local bar kind of loses its appeal when you have someone special right there at home." His gaze held hers and sheer joy shimmered through her.

Marion beamed down the length of the table at Ray. "Honey, please say the blessing. Everyone, join hands."

Amy offered one hand to Harrison. Derek took the other, his grip warm and firm. Ray said grace, amens echoed around the table and then everyone was talking at once, passing overflowing bowls and piled-high serving platters, dishing up the food.

Derek's hand brushed Amy's again, this time where it rested in her lap. She sent him a soft smile, turned her palm up and linked her fingers with his. Just long enough to share their own private moment with no one the wiser.

He had to pull away to serve himself a giant spoonful from the heaping bowl of mashed potatoes, but the warmth of his touch still lingered, soothing the old hurt for all the time they might have had together if things could have been different somehow.

Amy and Derek left the Armstrong house at half past eight. She followed him back to the Circle D.

They were barely in the door before he tossed his hat on the small entry table and grabbed her close.

His kiss…

Nothing compared to it.

She melted against him, her heart full of longing, her whole body burning, sparks of awareness popping and flashing all through her, her belly hollowing out, every inch of her skin on fire for him.

And then her phone rang.

She tried to ignore it, but Derek took her by the shoulders and pulled his thrilling, hot mouth from hers.

"Come back here." She slid her fingers up

into his hair and fisted them, surging up to claim those lips again.

But he just held on to her arms and stared in her eyes as the ringtone finally went silent. "That was your dad, am I right?"

She yanked the phone from the back pocket of her favorite jeans and dropped it on the narrow table next to Derek's discarded hat. "My dad can wait. I'll call him later." The voicemail alert chimed and she pretended not to hear it. "Now…" She slid her hands up over the crisp fabric of his shirt, enjoying the muscled strength in the hard flesh beneath. "Where were we?"

He just continued to stare down at her. "You ever call your mom back?"

Talk about a mood-killer. "I don't want to get into this." She dropped her hands and turned away.

But she didn't get far because he pulled her back. "You need to at least let them know that you're fine and you'll be in touch when you're ready."

"I don't need to do any such thing." She yanked free of his hold. "I'm thirty-one years old. It's up to me when and how I reach out to my parents." She turned on her heel and headed toward the great room.

"Thirty-one, huh?" He spoke to her retreating back. "Well, you're acting like a spoiled brat."

She whirled on him. "I don't want to talk to them right now."

He put up both hands. "Then don't talk to them. But let them know you're safe and well."

"Why are you worried about them? They've never been anything but mean to you."

He was trying not to grin. She could see the slight quiver at the corner of that sexy mouth of his. "They weren't *that* mean."

She let out a little growl of frustration. "I'm so mad at my dad for never telling me that he went after you that day, that he got you alone and worked on you. If he'd just stayed out of it—"

"What?" He raked his hands back through his beautiful, messy hair. "I mean, think about it. Yeah, he made it clear what he wanted and how he knew that what he wanted was right. But *we* made the decision, the two of us, you and me. You wanted to go—and I told you to go."

"But he didn't tell me what he did. For thirteen years, he didn't tell me. And he knew I was coming to town for the wedding, knew that I would be here for a whole month and that

I would more than likely run into you. And *still* he didn't tell me what I had a right to know. That's what I'm so angry about."

Derek picked up the phone and held it out to her. "A text. One sentence. 'I'm fine. Don't worry. I'll call you when I'm ready to talk.'"

"Actually..." she said, wrinkling her nose at him, "that's *three* sentences."

"Oh, come on, Amy. Can't you do that much for the poor guy who thinks the sun rises and sets on his little girl, and who's probably worried sick that you're dead in a ditch somewhere? Can't you just put his mind at ease?"

She wrapped her arms around her middle and fumed at him for a good fifteen seconds, feeling brattier and more mean-spirited as each second ticked by.

"Please," he said so very gently, melting her heart to a puddle of goo.

"Oh, all right." She marched back to him, grabbed the phone from his hand and typed out the exact three sentences he had suggested. "There." She held up the phone so he could read it for himself. "Satisfied?"

"Send it."

She hit the icon, closed the window and set the phone back down by his hat. "Now, I want you to make mad, passionate love to me, please. Do not make me hang around to see what he sends back."

"Deal." He took her hand, lifted it to his mouth and pressed his lips to the back of it. "God. You are so beautiful. All evening, at the Armstrongs', I kept thinking how I'm the guy who gets to bring you home."

Her pulse fluttered madly and her tummy got those butterflies—but she sulked anyway, as a matter of principle. "Flatter me all you want, but you kind of ruined the hot, sexy mood. You know that, right? You're going to have to make a serious effort to seduce me now, so stop fooling around and get to work."

He guided their joined hands around behind his back, pulling her up nice and close. He felt so warm and big and solid. And he smelled of leather and soap and that outdoorsy aftershave he favored. They had tonight and then one more week of nights. This impossible, wonderful time they'd agreed to be together was racing by much too fast.

"Just give me a chance," he teased.

"A chance for what?"

"To kiss it and make it all better." His rough, husky tone sent tendrils of heat curling down her spine.

She went on tiptoe, caught his earlobe between her teeth and gave it a tug, loving the low, needful sound he made in response. "Okay, you're forgiven. And yes, please, I would love it if you would kiss it and make it all better."

Her phone lit up, wrecking her mood all over again.

She glared up at him. "Don't ask me to check that."

"I wouldn't dare." He dropped a quick kiss on the end of her nose.

She unlaced their fingers and stepped back from him. Muttering a few choice words, she took the phone and brought up the text from her dad.

All right, then. Thanks for letting us know you're okay. Your mother and I send love.

She flashed the phone at Derek. "Happy now?" He just looked at her, all manly and tender, everything she'd ever wanted and lost somehow during the turbulent summer of her eighteenth year. "Grrr," she said, trying to drum up the outrage that kept draining away because he was so thoughtful and wonderful and good. "Ugh." And then she turned the phone back around and punched out, Love you, too, reading the words aloud in a sing-song as she typed them. "And..." She hit the little envelope icon. "Sent and done." And then she grabbed his hand and pulled him down the central hall, detouring to the right when she reached the open doorway that led to his bedroom.

Feeling like the luckiest man alive, Derek smoothed Amy's hair back and pressed a kiss to the flawless skin of her forehead. "You realize we have to be up by five at the latest." It was after midnight. They'd used two condoms and were discussing the wisdom of using a third. "We need to get some sleep."

"Yeah, I know." Her sigh was resigned. "Tomorrow's going to be a very busy day."

They still had to load his pickup and her Audi with the party stuff stored in his spare room. Bailey would bring everything that was still in the barn at Sunshine Farm. Everyone in the wedding party was on board to help—except the bride and the groom, who would have pitched in gladly if Amy would only allow that. Several other friends and family members had volunteered, as well.

They would all converge on Maverick Manor at 6:00 a.m. sharp. With everybody pitching in, Amy predicted they would have the setup complete by early afternoon.

She snuggled in closer to him, all gorgeous curves and velvet skin. He could hardly believe his good fortune, to have thirteen years' worth of dreams come true right here in his bed—for the next seven days, anyway.

Her breath brushed his neck and then her soft lips, too. She made a throaty, sexy little sound and traced his collarbone with a soft, lazy finger. "You feel so good. I love just touching you. Always. And forever. And even longer than that..."

Then stay with me. Never leave.

God. He wanted to say it.

But they'd only been together for a week. He needed to wait—at least until after the wedding. Then, one way or another, before she left for Boulder, he would ask her to consider a future for the two of them, ask her if maybe she might be willing to stay.

"Sleep." He settled her in closer and nuzzled her hair. It was everywhere, a net of silk, trailing over his shoulder, pooling against his bare chest, catching in his beard scruff that came in too fast no matter how often he shaved.

I love you...

For a moment, he was certain he'd said it

aloud and he didn't know whether to be glad that the words were out of his mouth after more than a decade of not being able to say them— or terrified that she might not take him seriously.

That could happen. He had to be ready for it. She could so easily say something gentle and regretful, about how they couldn't go there. How this was just a fling for as long as she was in town, how they both needed to accept this beautiful time together for what it was and not ruin a good thing.

Glad or terrified...

He didn't know which to be.

And he needed to stop obsessing about it. He wasn't going to say a thing about love and the future to her, anyway.

Not for another week yet, at least.

Chapter 9

"This party is perfect," Viv Shuster announced.

Amy beamed with pride. Things were going so well.

It was ten o'clock on Saturday night and the Jack and Jill bachelor party was in full swing. The guests, who added up to just about every adult in town and a lot of friends and family from other parts of the state and beyond, filled the public rooms of the gorgeous log cabin resort.

The last time Amy checked, every table in the casino room had been full. And in the giant, high-ceilinged lobby, the band played an upbeat Brad Paisley song and a lot of people were dancing, most of them wearing the straw cowboy hats offered at the door, hats decorated with a band of hearts and *Eva & Luke* written in glitter on a bigger heart where the crown met the brim. The Nearly Newlywed Game was a hit. Everyone seemed to be stepping up to bet on Luke and Eva's answers, dropping a buck in a giant pickle jar for each entry. The winner would go home with the pickle jar of dollar bills and a really nice bottle of champagne.

"To you and Derek, Amy." Viv raised her champagne flute high. "Just a completely amazing job."

"Thank you." Amy tapped her flute to Viv's. "I mean, you're the expert, so a high five from you is especially appreciated." And then she gave credit where it was due. "We had a lot of help. And the worksheets and suggestions you gave us definitely got us off to a great start."

Derek, every cowgirl's dream in dress jeans, fancy boots and a snow-white shirt, appeared out of the crowd and grabbed her hand. "Dance with me."

With a quick wave to Viv, she followed where he led her, to the windows that looked out on the Manor grounds. The wide square of open space there had been designated as the dance floor for the night.

They two-stepped and they line danced and during the slow ones, they held each other close. Amy could dance with him all night long.

But when the second slow song ended, she pulled away regretfully. "We should check on the games and make the rounds of the casino room."

"I'll take the casino," he said, and kissed her. Yes, it was breaking their no PDAs rule. So what? She kissed him back and didn't give a damn who saw. It was a bachelor party, after all, and the whole point was to break a few rules.

He headed for the casino and she wandered the other rooms, checking that the champagne station still had plenty of bubbly and the water table remained well stocked. She straightened the display at The Nearly Newlywed Game table.

And she entered the bar area just in time to see Brenna O'Reilly Dalton jump up onto her husband, Travis's, back. With a loud, "Wahoo!" Brenna wrapped her arms and legs around him. Amy laughed at the sight as Brenna tossed the bartender her phone so he could snap a picture of Travis running in a circle giving his wife a piggyback ride. It was one of the challenges in the Jack and Jill Scavenger Hunt. When the bartender returned her phone, Brenna passed it to Travis, who caught the shot as she kissed the bartender's cheek—another scavenger hunt challenge met.

Amy applauded, along with everyone nearby. Travis and Brenna were not only perfect together, they were both enthusiastic competitors. No wonder they'd stolen viewers' hearts on *The Great Roundup* reality TV show last year.

There was a tap on her shoulder. "Amy."

She turned to the bride-to-be, who looked absolutely gorgeous in a bright pink halter dress. "Eva! Love that dress. Having a good time?"

"Best. Time. Ever. And I have someone I've been wanting you to meet." Eva slipped her arm around the shoulders of a pretty dark-haired woman in a floral print maternity dress. "This is Mikayla Brown. She just arrived from Wyoming today and she'll be living with us at the farm for as long as we can convince her to stay."

Mikayla smiled, but her big, dark eyes remained watchful and serious. "Hi." She added kind of wearily, "Great party."

Eva's smooth brow crinkled. "Maybe I shouldn't have pushed you to come. Is it too much for you?"

"Of course not." Mikayla patted Eva's hand where it rested on her shoulder. "I feel fine and it's nice to get out and mix it up a little."

Dana Stockton, who'd arrived from Oregon two days ago, waved from down at the end of the bar where she sat with Bailey. "Eva! We need you!"

"Coming!" Eva turned to Mikayla. "That's Dana, Luke's youngest sister. I'll introduce you."

Mikayla put up a hand. "I'll meet her later. Go ahead and see what's up. I'm fine, really."

"You sure?"

"Positive."

Amy said, "Stick with me, Mikayla, I'll introduce you around—not that I know everyone, but I'm working on it."

"Terrific." Mikayla made shooing motions at Eva. "Go."

Eva took off to find out what Dana wanted and Amy offered, "Let's get you something cold to drink."

They each got a ginger ale and then wandered the party together. Amy kept an eye on the various events and refreshment tables, and made sure Mikayla met plenty of the locals, including Derek's brothers, Eli and Jonah. Eli introduced them to a bunch of Dalton cousins. Zach, Garrett, Shawn, Booker and Cole Dalton, Viv's fiancé, were the sons of Derek's uncle Phil. They all had thick dark hair and killer blue eyes.

Amy kidded, "You guys have my head spinning. There's a Dalton everywhere I turn."

Booker said, "And there are more on the way. Our Uncle Neal Dalton is moving to town along with his boys Morgan, Holt and Boone." He leaned close to Amy and stage-whispered, "Take my word on this, Amy. You gotta watch your back around Uncle Neal's boys."

"Come on, Booker," said Eli, frowning. "They're not *that* bad."

Booker scoffed. "They're bad enough," he muttered. "But you're right. I should shut up and go find another beer."

Amy took Mikayla's arm. "Let's see how it's going in the casino."

The casino room, done up like a saloon in an old Western movie, was wall-to-wall with guests shooting craps, playing poker and rummy, baccarat and blackjack.

Derek had gotten stuck filling in as croupier at the roulette table. He called out "Place your bets!" and then spun the wheel, which Amy had picked up for practically nothing on eBay. After he paid the winners, he glanced over and gave Amy a wink, causing her pulse to speed up and her heart to do the happy dance. All the Dalton boys were handsome, but Derek really was the best-looking of all of them. Everyone said so, and everyone was right.

"Let me guess," said Mikayla. "That's your guy."

"Oh, yes, he is." And then she remembered the agreement they'd made. "Correction." She couldn't help giggling. "We're just friends."

"Oh, yeah. And if you think I believe that, I've got a uranium mine I can sell you." The golden light from the wagon wheel chandelier overhead put tired shadows under Mikayla's big dark eyes.

Amy took her arm. "Come on. Let's go someplace more comfortable where we can sit down for a while."

They went outside and found an unoccupied bench waiting for them under the star-filled Montana sky.

Mikayla set her empty glass on the ground beside her and sat back with a little sigh. "It's nice out here."

"Yeah. Just right." The evening was warm,

with a hint of a breeze. "So, you're from Wyoming, Eva said?"

"Cheyenne, specifically." Mikayla stared off down the twisting path that led deeper into the resort grounds. "Luke and my cousin Brent are longtime friends. Before Luke came back here to Montana, he and Brent both had jobs on the same big spread not far from Cheyenne. As for me, the past few years, I've been working at a day care. My job ended several weeks ago and I...needed a change of scenery, I guess you could say. Brent called Luke. Luke said I should come stay at Sunshine Farm. So here I am, with the room next to yours, according to Eva. Till the baby's born, anyway. Maybe longer. I really can't say."

"Knowing Eva and Luke, they'll be glad to have you for as long as you want to stay. They're the best."

"Yes, they are." Mikayla folded her hands on the mound of her belly.

For a few minutes, they were quiet together, a companionable sort of silence. Amy could hear the sounds of the party from back inside the Manor, the band playing a ballad, people laughing and chatting.

Then Mikayla said softly, "You might have guessed that I'm on my own with this." Her dark head was tipped down and she stroked her stomach as though soothing the little one within. "The father…well, I kind of made a bad choice with him. Long story short, he cheated. I wanted more than a guy who couldn't even be true to me. I wanted love. *Real* love. The kind that curls your toes and fills your heart and lasts till the day after the end of forever."

Amy thought of Derek, of their not-quite-baby, of how much he'd wanted to marry her, of the love and hope in his beautiful green eyes when he'd dropped to his knees and begged her to be his wife. Even though it all spiraled into heartbreak later, she'd been so lucky with him—*was* so lucky with him.

Whatever happened between them now, she would always know that Derek Dalton, the first love she'd never really gotten over, was a hero in the truest sense of the word.

She said, "Good riddance on the cheater."

"Thank you," Mikayla replied dryly. "I couldn't agree more."

"And you won't be on your own for long, believe me. Everybody will tell you that Rust Creek Falls is the place to come if you're looking for the love of your life."

Mikayla let out a husky laugh. "Well, I *was* looking and it didn't go well. Now it's me and my baby and you know what? That's just fine with me."

Amy glanced toward the Manor. As though her yearning heart had conjured him, Derek emerged. Every molecule in her body lit up at the sight of him. She waved. He saw her and came toward them.

Mikayla said, "Here comes that 'friend' of yours. Go on, now. Dance and have fun."

Amy held out her hand. "Come with us."

But Mikayla shook her head. "Uh-uh. Go. Dance. And have a glass of bubbly for me."

Amy did dance. And not only with Derek. She danced with Bella's multimillionaire husband, Hudson Jones, and his equally rich brothers: Walker—who was married to Derek's cousin, Lindsay—and Gideon and Jensen who were visiting from out of town. She danced with the Strickland boys, L.J., Trey, Benjamin and Billy, who lived in Thunder Canyon. She also danced with their brother Drew Strickland, an obstetrician. Rumor had it that Drew might soon be moving to Rust Creek Falls.

She even danced with Collin Traub as his wife, Willa, danced with Derek. Collin was friendly and kind. He said what a great job she and Derek had done on the party and not so much as a word about what he knew of the past.

Much later, after two in the morning when the party was slowly winding down, when her poor feet were aching from hours of dancing, Amy took off her high-heeled sandals and ran barefoot with Derek along the twisting paths on the Maverick Manor grounds.

"Wait," he said, his boots going still. "Listen."

She paused in midstep—and she heard it, too. Slow and sweet in the distance, back in the Manor, the band was playing, "Hey, Pretty Girl."

Derek reeled her in and pulled her close. "I believe this dance is mine."

She gazed up into his eyes. They gleamed in the darkness, endlessly deep. "Yes, this dance is yours, Derek. All yours."

And he whirled her around under the moon in a pool of starlight. It was pure magic. Her tired feet had never felt so light, as though she was floating right off the ground.

At four thirty in the morning, when the last guest finally left the party, Amy changed into the jeans, T-shirt and trusty high-tops she'd brought along to wear for the cleanup.

She and Derek and Luke's brothers stayed on to help the staff break everything down. Nate Crawford and his partners in the resort would be keeping all the props and decorations. Amy and Derek were happy to give the Manor every last poster, banner and baggie of wedding ring confetti. They had no use for any of it and the Manor had been beyond generous, letting them use the venue for nearly nothing. The owners planned to host a lot of parties in the future. Decorations and party props and a ready-to-assemble saloon-themed casino would be bound to come in handy.

As the sun peeked over the crests of the mountains and lit up the morning sky, she followed Derek back to the Circle D. All night, she'd been looking forward to getting him alone. Every dance they'd shared had reminded her of how precious this time was— *their* time, together again at last. She couldn't wait to unzip his jeans, pull off his fancy boots and unbutton that snowy white shirt.

When they finally got to his place, it was eight in the morning. They'd both been awake since 5:00 a.m. the day before. She turned off the engine of her Audi and then just sat there in the driver's seat, staring blankly out the windshield.

The sun was fully above the mountains now, the sky so clear and pure and blue. About fifty yards away, a couple of horses had ambled up to the fence that ran along the dirt road leading off toward the main house. They shook their manes, snorting and whinnying and then wheeled and took off back the way they had come.

Such a beautiful place—Rust Creek Falls, the mountains all around, the wide, rolling valley. She'd stayed away much too long. Being back felt so good. It felt like coming home.

She heard the pickup door open and close and then boots crunching gravel.

Derek leaned in her open window. "You're dead on your feet."

A laugh bubbled up and she corrected him, "I'm dead on my butt is what I am."

He pulled open her door. "Come here, pretty girl."

She fell sideways out the door, still laughing. He caught her—and suddenly, her throat was tight, her vision blurred with tears. She wrapped her arms around his neck as he scooped her high against his chest. "Oh, Derek. We killed it, didn't we? It was a great party."

"The best ever," he answered solemnly. She tipped her head back enough to see his eyes under the brim of his hat. His brow furrowed. "You're crying. What'd I do?"

She snuggled her head under his chin, her hair catching on his beard scruff the way it always did. "This is happy crying," she explained, causing him to mutter something about women and all the ways a man could never understand them. She pressed her hand against his shirt, right over his heart. "Honestly, I am happy. So very happy—and I waited all night to get this shirt off you."

His lips touched her hair. "Let's go inside and you can get busy on that."

She reached out and pushed her door shut. He turned for the steps leading up to the porch.

Inside, he carried her straight to the bedroom.

When he set her down, she fell back across the bed, arms outstretched. "Gonna close my eyes, just for a minute…"

"Yeah." She heard the warm humor in his voice as he untied her shoes. "You do that, Miss Wainwright."

"I believe I will, thank you very much." She let her heavy eyelids drift shut and thought about all the naughty things she would do to him. Sexy things. Delicious things.

It was going to be so much fun…

* * *

When she woke, she was alone in the bed wearing only her lacy panties and bra from the night before. The nightstand clock said 4:00 p.m.

"Derek?"

No answer. And the house felt strangely silent.

She saw the note sticking out from under the clock.

Gone to round up some stray cattle. My mom called. She says we're going to dinner at main house. Just casual. Be back for you by six at the latest.

Back when she and Derek were high school sweethearts, Amy had been to more than one Sunday dinner at Charles and Rita Dalton's house. She remembered the rambling, two-story ranch house. In those days, Sunday dinners were crowded, every chair taken.

But all of Derek's brothers and sisters were married now and none of them had come to Sunday dinner this particular evening. It was just Derek, Amy, Rita and Charles.

Derek's parents seemed happy to see her. They asked about her life in Boulder and her work for Hurdly and Main. Charles seemed pretty interested in how she tracked financial fraudsters on the internet. Rita listened politely, but her eyes got that glassy look, the one most people ended up wearing when she tried to explain about stopping data breaches and the lengths some tech-savvy crooks would go to steal what didn't belong to them.

Rita plied her with roast beef, broccoli and cheesy potatoes and asked, "Have you been to the saddlery?"

"Yes. Derek gave me a tour."

"Isn't he talented?"

"Mom," Derek groaned. "Don't."

Rita gave him her sweetest smile. "Well, I'm your mother. I'm allowed to be impressed with you."

"His work is beautiful," Amy said, and meant it.

"He's an artist," Rita declared with pride. "He gets commissions, did you know that? From people in Europe, from all over the world. And they pay a *lot*."

"Mom." Derek pinned his mother with a flinty stare. "Stop. I gave Amy a tour of the shop and I told her all about it."

Charles chuckled and Rita ate a bite of tender beef.

"So, Amy," Rita said when she'd finished

chewing and swallowing. "It's wonderful to have you back in town, to hear that you've been spending time with Derek again. I always thought that the two of you—"

"Mom," Derek said for the third time, the single syllable freighted with warning.

Rita widened her eyes, all innocence. "What I meant to say was, I hope we're going to be seeing a lot of you."

"Well, I'll be here until the wedding, that's for sure."

"And after that?"

Amy couldn't stop her glance from sliding to Derek. For a moment, their gazes locked. She dared to think he wanted her to stay, that when they finally really talked about it after the wedding, they would be discussing how to blend their two lives into one. "I...ahem. I guess you never know what will happen, do you?"

Rita arched an eyebrow. "You're a cagey one, Amy Wainwright."

"Leave her alone, Mom," Derek said.

Rita sighed. "It's a thankless job, being a mother. Your children grow up and they won't tell you anything."

Charles reached over and put his hand on his wife's. "Be patient, my love."

Rita leaned his way and kissed him. "All right, then." She smoothed her napkin on her lap and picked up her fork again. "Don't mind me, Amy. I'm just glad to have you here again at last."

The next week just plain didn't have enough hours in it. It felt like a whirlwind, with the wedding coming up and all the Armstrongs in town.

Monday, Eva and her bridesmaids drove into Kalispell for their final fittings. It was Amy, Eva, Delphine and Calla, plus Luke's sisters, Bella and Dana, and his sisters-in-law, Fallon and Annie. They took over the wedding boutique and shared champagne and snacks as they tried on their dresses for the big day.

They snapped selfies like mad. The full-length gowns were gorgeous, each one in a different color and style. They'd all brought the cowboy boots they would be wearing on the big day. At first, Eva had wanted them in dressy nude pumps, but the boots were a better choice for a barn wedding, especially with the ceremony itself being held outside on uneven scrub grass.

When Eva tried on her dress, all the happy laughter and chatter stopped. She emerged from the dressing room and everybody sighed. Her sleeveless gown had a fitted bodice and a full skirt of ruffled tulle, and it was perfect with her teal-blue, white-tooled cowboy boots.

"You are a vision," Calla said reverently at last. They all burst into enthusiastic applause and more than a few tears.

The next day, Amy went with Eva to check in with Viv. The lists of things still to do before the wedding went on and on.

"Don't forget to break in those pretty cowboy boots," Viv advised. "Get plenty of sleep. Practice your vows out loud. Keep on top of your email just in case someone has something important they have to tell you about their part in the wedding. Pack your honeymoon bags well ahead and check them the next day to make sure you haven't forgotten anything. Confirm that Derek has his toast prepared, and your dad. As for the cake—"

Eva cut her off. "I have the cake completely under control."

"I just worry it's too much for you. You're the *bride*."

Eva stood taller. "Yes, I am. The bride who happens to be a baker by profession. I've always dreamed of baking my own wedding cake and that is exactly what I'm doing."

Viv had the good sense not to argue the point further. She turned to Amy. "How about your toast?"

"I'm on it," Amy promised, her fingers crossed behind her back.

That night, she and Derek worked together on the toasts. She helped him write his and he gave her a few great pointers on hers. And then they went to bed and stayed awake too late, making love, whispering together, laughing a lot. At one in the morning, they got up and raided the freezer. They ate cappuccino-chunky-chocolate ice cream straight from the carton and then went back to bed and made love again.

Suddenly, it was Wednesday.

Before accompanying Eva to a final check-in with the caterer, Amy had a long Skype meeting with her supervisor and his boss at Hurdly and Main. It took some convincing, but they finally agreed that it didn't matter whether she worked from her home in Boulder or in Montana. They said they would want her at the Boulder office for a few days a month, minimum, and to remain available several times a year to give expert testimony when certain cases she'd developed ended up in court.

She signed off the Skype call knowing she

could make her job work long-distance and she couldn't wait to get with Derek and talk it over.

But then she started thinking how that would be jumping the gun a little. After the wedding, that was the time to discuss whatever might happen next. They would talk then about their desires and intentions for the future. That would be the time to tell him she could tele-commute, the time to prove how much she wanted to be with him by showing him how she was prepared to make that happen.

Thursday, during the two hours she spent at Sunshine Farm supposedly working, she picked up her phone out of the blue and called her father.

"Jelly Bean, I'm so happy to hear your voice."

Jelly Bean. The silly nickname made her tear up a little. She could hear his love for her in the way he said it and right now, she didn't want to feel his love. She wanted to yell at him for the things he'd done thirteen years ago—the things he'd done and never copped to. "Hey, Dad."

"Still in Rust Creek Falls?"

"That's right."

"Having a good time?"

She had no idea where to even start with

him. So, she came right out with it. "Dad, I'm in love with Derek Dalton and I always have been and I'm going to give it my whole heart this time around. I'm not positive how it will work out yet, but my plan is to move back here and make a life with him." *That is, if he wants a life with me.*

The silence was deafening. "I see," Jack Wainwright said at last. "What about your job?"

"I've handled that. I work mostly from home anyway. It's not going to be a big deal. And Dad, I'm telling you this because I want you to know how I feel and how I hope things will work out. Don't you dare approach Derek behind my back."

For a long count of five, her father said nothing. Then, at last, he answered quietly, "I won't."

"Promise?"

"I do." There was another endless silence, after which he shocked the hell out of her by saying, "Your mother and I had a feeling this might happen, that with a month back in Montana, you and Derek would...reconnect. I expected this. And I'm glad. Your mother will be, too."

A silly sputtering sound escaped her. She stammered, "Wh-what did you just say?"

"I said I'm glad and I meant it. I know you really loved that boy."

"*Love*, Dad. Present tense."

"All right. *Love* him, then. I know you love him and over the years, I've regretted my role in tearing you two apart. I've realized we could have found a better way, a way for you to get the education you deserved and still be with the boy you love."

Tears clogged her throat and burned her eyes—and that made her furious. "I've talked to Derek about that summer. He finally admitted that you came to find him at the Circle D, that you begged him to let me go."

Her dad said simply, "That's true."

"Why didn't you even have the integrity to tell me what you did?"

"It's hard to explain…"

"Try me," she insisted through clenched teeth.

"Well, at first, I thought the main thing was to get you away from him and Rust Creek Falls, to get you back to focusing on your education, on your new life in Boulder. But then, over time, I felt guilty. I knew that at the very least, you did have a right to know that I had convinced your boyfriend—"

"Husband, Dad. Derek was my husband."

And the father of the child I never had. She considered just saying it, confessing that last sad little truth right out loud.

But her dad didn't need to know, not really. And bringing up the baby now would only confuse the issue at hand.

"Yes," said her dad. "Derek was your husband. I know. And I promise you, Amy, at the time I thought I was doing the right thing for you."

"Well, it *wasn't* right."

"I see that now. But it seemed right at the time. And later, over time, I saw the sadness in you. I saw that what you felt for Derek really did run deep. And somehow, I just never could find the words to tell you what I'd done. Then every year I didn't tell you, it only got harder to decide how to come out with it, how to admit to you that I'd convinced Derek that if he really loved you, the only choice was to let you go."

If he really loved me... All her anger just leached away. She felt only sadness, for what was lost, what might have been. "So. I guess he really did love me, huh?"

"Yes, sweetheart. I believe he really did—and still does, from what you're telling me now."

Oh, she did hope so.

"Maybe in time you'll come to forgive me," her father said.

Of course, she would forgive him. But some stubborn part of her refused to make it too easy for him. "I'm not happy with you about this."

"I understand."

"But, Dad, I do love you. Mom, too."

"And we love you. So much. We just want you to be happy, that's all. Please tell Derek I look forward to seeing him again, to having a chance to apologize in person for the wrong I did him thirteen years ago."

"I'll tell him."

They said goodbye, after which she sat staring blankly at her computer monitor, longing to tell Derek everything her dad had just said.

And she *would* tell him, once the wedding was over and it was finally time to talk about the rest of their lives.

Chapter 10

Friday afternoon, the wedding party gathered and did the walk-through outside under the clear, sunny sky, in front of the big, wideopen doors of the yellow barn. That evening, Bella and Hudson hosted the rehearsal dinner at their house.

Amy and Derek didn't get back to his place until after midnight. They were so close now to the end of their friends-with-secret-benefits agreement. After tomorrow, it would happen at last. They would talk about the future, decide what came next for them.

If anything, she thought and shivered a little. But that was just fatalism rearing its ugly head.

She wasn't going to be negative. Uh-uh. Because she definitely believed they did have a future, she and Derek. She wanted it so much. And she was almost positive that he wanted it, too.

She longed to get going on it, get her dreams for the future out in the open. But really, the best thing at this point, she decided, was to stick with the plan, to get through the wedding tomorrow, to enjoy the party afterward.

And then, over breakfast Sunday morning, she would do it. She would tell him that she loved him, that she'd realized now she'd never stopped. She would say she wanted another chance with him. She wanted to stay here in Rust Creek Falls with him and get busy on the rest of their lives.

"You're really quiet," he said, holding her close after they'd climbed into bed.

She wavered. Why not just tell him everything right now?

But in the end, she chickened out. "I keep going over my toast in my head. I hope I get it right."

"It's a great little speech," he soothed, stroking her hair.

"Little is right. Because short is always best." *And I love you and I want it to work out for us this time. At last. Oh, Derek. I want that so bad...*

"It's gonna be fine," he promised, catching a random curl and wrapping it around his finger.

She lifted her chin and captured his gaze. "You sure?"

"No doubt." His eyes were bottle-green in the light of the bedside lamp, and beneath the covers, she felt him stirring, growing hard against her bare hip. He said her name, "Amy," like a promise. Or a plea. His wonderful mouth dipped down and claimed hers.

She kissed him back with all the love and yearning in her heart.

It was going to work out this time.

It *had* to work out.

There was no other possibility but happiness for them now. After all these long years apart, they deserved to share a future together. And Sunday morning, over coffee and pancakes, they would start planning the rest of their lives.

At three o'clock the next afternoon, beneath the blue Montana sky, the groomsmen and the groom took their places at the makeshift altar in front of the yellow barn. The six-piece band launched into the traditional wedding march and the bridesmaids, in a rainbow of bright dresses, took their walk down the aisle. They carried bouquets of sunflowers and lavender phlox. As the maid of honor, Amy came last.

When she took her place with the other bridesmaids, three cherubs appeared—Jamie Stockton's two-and-a-half-year-old triplets, Jared, Henry and Kate. Kate came first in a ruffled blush-pink dress, tiny cowboy boots on her feet. She scattered petals as she went. Jared and Henry, the ring bearers, were right behind her, perfect little cowboys in jeans, boots, blue shirts, tan vests and hats to match. The three made it almost to the bridal party assembled at the end of the aisle.

But a few feet from their destination, something caught Henry's eye. "Horsie!" he cried, veering off at the end of the white carpet and racing toward a gray gelding standing at the pasture fence twenty yards away. A murmur of laughter rose from the guest.

Fallon, the triplets' stepmother, moved fast. She caught little Henry before he made good his escape. Jamie corralled Jared, just in case he got ideas from his brother. Kate never wavered. She took her place with the rest of the wedding party, head high, her angelic face composed.

Then the music changed, and a lone guitarist

played Pachelbel's *Canon in D*. More than one pair of eyes brimmed with tears as Eva, a vision in white except for the teal-blue toes of her cowboy boots peeking out beneath her skirt, her bright hair covered in a filmy veil, emerged from the bride's tent set up a few yards from the foot of the white carpet. She carried sunflowers, purple phlox, white roses and yellow snapdragons.

Not far from the tent, Ray Armstrong waited. He offered Eva his arm and whispered something to her. She murmured a reply. Even through her veil, her pretty face seemed to glow.

Ray walked his youngest daughter down the aisle, stepping aside at last to leave her facing her groom. A sigh went up from the rows of white chairs as Luke turned back her veil.

Their eyes only for each other, they said their vows and exchanged their rings. Then, as Luke kissed his bride, Amy's gaze strayed to Derek. He was already watching her. They shared a secret smile.

Tomorrow. The word echoed in her head.

Tomorrow would be their day, hers and Derek's. She couldn't wait to tell him everything, to open her heart to him, to claim again what they'd lost all those years ago.

For the wedding dinner and reception, Viv Shuster had worked a miracle in the old barn, with twinkle lights and long plank tables. She'd hung gorgeous old crystal chandeliers from the overhead beams and created a bower effect with yards of filmy white fabric draped from the rafters. There were flowers in mason jars everywhere.

It really was perfect, Amy thought. Eva had never looked so radiant, so gloriously happy.

As for Derek, he was sweet and attentive. But as the afternoon became early evening, he seemed to grow distracted—distant, even. As though something was preying on his mind.

Derek couldn't quite put his finger on what was bugging him. A lot of things, really. Amy had been too quiet the last couple of days. He wasn't sure what was going on with her, but it kind of made him nervous.

He had hopes, he really did, for a future with her. And he'd made a secret trip to Kalispell two days before because this time, he intended to offer something a whole lot better than an imitation diamond when he made his big move. But maybe he'd jumped the gun.

Maybe she was only thinking that it was almost time for her to go.

Or maybe it was this perfect country wedding messing with his head. It was like a dream, with Luke and Eva so happy, their whole lives ahead of them and nothing standing in their way. And it reminded him too painfully of how different his own wedding day had been, of him and Amy at the courthouse with strangers for witnesses, of the forty-dollar wedding ring and the tired-looking bunch of daisies she'd clutched in her hand as they vowed to love and care for each other as long as they both should live.

This wedding brought all the old hurts to fresh life again, reminding him how much he'd loved her and how wrong it all went, how little he'd had to offer her then.

His plan was to speak of the future with her tomorrow, to tell her he still loved her and always would. How was that going to go? He couldn't be sure what she'd say when he asked her to be his again in front of the world—forever this time, no matter what.

He tried to take heart from the tender looks she gave him, but playing the "just friends" game was really getting to him. He hated it now. He wanted to shout to the world that she was his. That they were together.

At dinner, it was open seating for everyone

but the bride and groom, who sat at a smaller table up on a dais. Derek and Amy sat together. He rested his arm across the back of her chair and she didn't remind him that he was pushing the boundaries of their friends-only act.

Instead, she leaned close to him and whispered how handsome he looked in his jeans and dress boots, his blue shirt and tan vest. She even straightened his white rose boutonniere, the way a woman does for her special guy.

He was feeling pretty good about everything, gaining confidence about how it would go between them tomorrow when he asked her for forever.

But then Brandi Foster, who lived in Kalispell but sometimes spent her Friday nights at the Ace, pulled out a chair across the table from them. "Derek! How have you been?" She raised her mason jar of wedding punch. "Been a while, huh?"

Yes, it had. About five years, if he wasn't mistaken. They'd hooked up at the Ace one Friday or Saturday night back when he was spending too much time meeting women in bars. She'd given him her number before he left her place. He'd never gotten around to calling her back.

"Hi, Brandi," he said, going through the

motions, being polite. "I'm doing well. How 'bout you?"

"Can't complain." She kind of scowled as she said it. Her gaze shifted to Amy. "If it isn't the maid of honor. I'm Brandi." She offered her hand across the table.

Amy took it and gave it a quick shake.

Brandi had a million questions for Amy. Did she live in town? Oh, well, then, if she didn't, where *did* she live and when was she going back? How did she know Eva? And no kidding, she went to high school in Rust Creek Falls and graduated the same year as Derek? "So, you were schoolmates, you two."

"Yes, we were." Amy leaned a little closer to him and sent him a fond smile. The warmth in those golden-green eyes eased the knot of tension gathering in the center of his chest. Amy didn't seem all that bothered to be fielding endless questions from a woman she didn't know.

But then Brandi snickered and drank more punch. The tension in Derek's chest fisted tight again. Brandi seemed a little buzzed. He wondered if eccentric old Homer Gilmore, famous for spiking the punch at weddings with his dangerously powerful moonshine, might be up to his old tricks again. Brandi craned across the table and stage-whispered to Amy, "Well, if you went to school with Derek, I guess I don't have to warn you about him."

Amy only shrugged. "Of course not. I'm sure I know him a lot better than you do."

Brandi tossed her blond head. "Oh, you think so, huh?"

"I *know* so."

Brandi grabbed her empty mason jar and swept to her feet. "Just don't expect a phone call afterward, if you know what I'm saying. I need more punch." She turned and flounced away without giving Amy a chance to say anything more.

Amy sent him a sideways look. "I get the impression that Brandi is not very happy with you."

Feeling like a first-class jerk, he eased his arm off the back of her chair. "Yeah. Well, she's right. I never did call her."

"How long ago was this?"

"Five years or so."

She leaned in and nudged his shoulder with hers. "Come on. Don't beat yourself up. It was a long time ago and everybody just needs to move on."

God, she was amazing, the way she took the awkward, ugly encounter in stride. He dipped his head to hers and whispered, "Thanks."

She caught his hand under the table. "Hey. It's okay." She wove their fingers together, her eyes steady on his, letting him know that Brandi hadn't bothered her in the least.

It helped, her kind words, her soft hand in his. But not enough, really.

Brandi was living proof of what a dog he'd once been and that made him feel…less. Cheap. Like he wasn't quite good enough, somehow.

He really needed to buck up. Take Amy's advice and shake it the hell off.

Dinner was served. And then it was time for the toasts. Derek thought his went over well enough.

Amy's was so sweet and funny. She had great stories about Eva as a little girl who followed Calla, Delphine and Amy around the Armstrong backyard, asking a thousand questions: *How do you know when you're in love? Does a girl need a good job before she gets married? I know you're all bigger than me and teenagers and everything—but still, can we please play My Little Pony and can I be Princess Twilight Sparkle?*

After the toasts and dinner, there was dancing at one end of the barn. People lingered at the tables or wandered around outside, where the white folding chairs and rows of hay bales provided plenty of seating. The sun sank below the mountains and the outside party lights came on, endless strings of them, looped between the exterior walls of the barn and the nearby trees.

Derek and Amy stayed together. They danced and they visited with friends and family. He was having a great time and had almost forgotten the depressing encounter with Brandi.

But then, after dark, as they sat together on a hay bale under the loops of lights, a guy he didn't know wandered over.

"Hey. You're Amy, right?" He offered his hand to her and they shook. "And…?" He turned to Derek.

Derek stood. "Derek Dalton."

The guy shook his hand, too. But his attention remained on Amy. "I'm Joe Armstrong, Eva's cousin. Uncle Ray's my dad's brother."

Amy got up, too. "Marion has talked about you."

Joe grinned. "All good stuff, right?"

"Absolutely. She said you live in Denver."

Joe was a good-looking guy if you liked the executive type. He wore a pricey suit and tie—and cowboy boots. It was a barn wedding, after all. A guy never knew what he might step in. "I'm an attorney," he said, "with Bartles, Downey and Smart. Ray said you live in Boulder."

"For the past several years, yes."

"We should get together." Joe whipped out a phone bigger than Amy's. "Give me your number or an email." Derek wanted to punch the fool. "Or wait. Are you on LinkedIn?"

Amy started to say something. But before she got an actual word out, Derek took a step forward. "Back off." The warning was out before he let himself think twice about how rude he sounded or what Joe-freaking-Armstrong might think.

Joe almost dropped his enormous phone. "Hey. Whoa, there." He actually put up both hands like Derek had a gun on him. "No offense, man. Seriously."

Derek knew himself to be a jealous fool. He stuck his hands in his pockets to keep them from grabbing good old Joe by the throat. "Sorry. That was out of line."

"Derek?" Amy sounded worried.

Joe muttered something in a neutral tone.

But Derek didn't hear it. He needed a serious time-out—like go sit in a corner with his face to the wall. Spinning on his heel, he walked away.

"Derek!" She was coming after him.

He felt like crap and just wanted to go. But no way could he leave her like that, calling his name, trying to catch up with him. He stopped and waited under the night-shadowed branches of a hackberry tree.

She ducked in there beneath the leaves with him. "Derek? Are you okay?"

He had so much to say to her and no idea where to start.

Not that this was the time or the place for it.

The least he could do was apologize. "I... look, I really am sorry. I'm an ass and I don't know what the hell's the matter with me."

Cautiously, moving with slow care, like someone soothing a spooked horse, she brushed her palm along his arm. Her touch soothed him. He got a hint of her perfume and relaxed a little more.

When he didn't pull away, she stepped in close. "We, um, have a lot to talk about. Maybe we should—"

"Not now." He just wasn't ready. And what if she said no? Through the darkness her eyes gleamed so bright. "I'm sorry, I really am. I don't know what I was thinking to jump on that guy like that."

Her pretty white teeth flashed with her

smile. "Well, Ray's nephew seems a little pushy. But I think he's harmless, really."

"I got jealous." There. He'd admitted it, even though it made him look like even more of an ass.

"Don't be. I've got no interest in getting anything going with Ray's nephew. You're the only one I'm looking at."

"Even when I act like an idiot?"

"You're not an idiot. No way." Her gaze didn't waver. "You're the best man I know."

"Well, I *am* the best man," he teased lamely and tugged on a loose curl of her pinned-up hair. "You're kind. A good woman."

"It's only the truth." She caught his fingers, brought them to her lips and pressed a kiss into his palm.

He could have stayed there under that tree with her forever, just looking into her big eyes, feeling her velvety cheek against his hand. But the evening wasn't over yet. "We should go back. They haven't even cut the cake."

"You sure you're okay?"

He traced the curve of her ear, ran the back of his finger down the side of her throat—and for no logical reason, out of nowhere, the hard things Collin had said that morning at the saddlery filled his mind.

Guys like you and me, we go from girl to girl. And people judge us. They think we haven't got deep feelings. But could be it's the opposite. Maybe our feelings run too damn deep...

You were wrecked over her. That girl ruined you. I didn't understand then, how deep she'd cut you...

Back in the barn, the band was playing "Lost in This Moment," that Big & Rich song about getting married. Would he ever get there again with the only woman for him?

Yesterday, he'd believed he would. But somehow, tonight, with Luke and Eva's happiness reminding him of how it all went wrong before, with tomorrow coming on too fast, he just didn't know anymore.

"Derek?" There was worry in her eyes again.

"I'm good," he lied. "Never better."

They went back to the party. They danced some more. They hung out with Derek's brothers and sisters and their wives and husbands.

Eva and Luke eventually got down to cutting the gorgeous cake that Eva had insisted on baking herself. It was enormous, that cake, a tower of white frosting and twining frosting flowers, with a cowgirl bride and her cowboy groom perched on top. Inside, the cake itself was yellow swirled with bright ribbons of raspberry filling.

Amy and Derek sat inside at one of the tables to shovel it in.

Bailey strolled up with a giant slice of his own. He took the place across from Amy. "You two." He smirked at them. "Worst kept secret in Rust Creek Falls." He pointed with his fork at Amy, then at Derek. "I can't believe it's really happened. I never thought it would. But it looks to me like Derek Dalton has finally met his match."

Derek slid a glance at Amy. She was grinning. He looked back at Bailey and played his part, deadpan. "No idea what you're talkin' about, man."

"Oh, give me a break." Bailey stuck a big bite of cake in his mouth, chewed it and swallowed before continuing, "You two are together and you're fooling nobody."

Amy laughed. "Are you kidding?" And then, cool as the middle of a long winter's night, she said, "No, we are not together, no way."

The hair on the back of Derek's neck stood up. *She's dumping you tomorrow, fool*, said a flat voice inside his head. *She's just playing her part, playing the friend game.*

What was he, blind? It was all right there in front of him and he needed to open his damn eyes and look at the truth: *her laugh, that cold way she'd said that we aren't together...*

Derek knew then with absolute certainty that he'd read this situation all wrong, that he'd been thinking forever but she wasn't thinking about anything but right now and she never had been.

She'd been honest with him from the first. *Friends with secret benefits.* That was what they were.

It was *all* that they were.

And what about Joe Armstrong? The more he thought about the way she'd acted when Ray's nephew put the move on her, the more he thought that just maybe she was kind of interested in that guy.

Yeah, she'd run after him when he took off like some little boy with a big crush who couldn't handle his own damn feelings. But that was because she had a kind heart. In a situation like that, she would have run to offer comfort to anyone.

Bottom line: she was just waiting for the damn wedding to be over so she could get back to Boulder and her real life.

What did he have to offer a girl like her? A little house on the family ranch, an ordinary life in the small town she'd left behind years ago.

Past and present were all mixed up together, suddenly. He'd had this dream of a certain girl and now was the part where the dream turned to a nightmare. It had hurt so bad to lose her last time.

And now it was about to happen all over again.

The evening wore on, the party lights twinkling, the band playing one corny love song after another, everyone laughing and chattering, just happy to be there as Eva and Luke claimed a lifetime together.

"You're quiet," she said, same as he'd said last night. They were dancing to Jason Aldean's "Staring at the Sun" and he wished from the bottom of his soul that the damn band could play something that wasn't about loving a woman forever.

He didn't answer her, just pulled her closer and leaned his cheek against her soft, sweet-smelling hair and wished that the end wasn't coming on so damn fast.

"Derek, I have so much I want to—"

"Shh," he whispered. He kissed the tender indentation just below her temple and pulled her closer still. "Just dance with me. Just dance..."

She made the sweetest, softest little sound and rested her head on his shoulder. They danced on.

At midnight, Eva climbed up to the hayloft to throw her bouquet. All the single women—and more than a few girls nowhere near old enough to get married—gathered beneath the hayloft doors, each one eager to make the catch.

Derek stood with the men, watching the age-old ritual, listening to Bailey grouse about ridiculous traditions.

"Wait!" Amy called from the middle of the tight knot of women.

Above, Eva laughed. "What now?"

"Where's Mikayla? I don't see Mikayla!"

Eva held her bouquet high. "Go get her, Amy. I'll wait. She's not missing this chance."

Amy wriggled free of the jostling crowd of eager females. "Mikayla!" she hollered.

The very pregnant little brunette stepped reluctantly forward. "This is just silly."

But Amy only grabbed her hand and dragged her into the middle of the crowd of women and girls. "Ready!" she shouted to Eva when she had Mikayla where she wanted her.

Derek looked up to the loft and saw Eva turn around as though to throw the flowers blind. But at the last second, she whirled front again and threw them straight for Amy's outstretched hands.

With a whoop of triumph, Amy seemed to catch them—but then everyone was laughing and shouting. The knot of women loosened and he saw it.

There was Mikayla in the center of the circle with the flowers clutched tightly in her hands.

Yeah, okay, Derek knew it was only an old superstition. No woman really got married next just because she ended up with the flowers that had been the bride's.

But still, women fought to make that catch. Amy hadn't. Instead, she'd made sure that Mikayla got lucky.

Because Amy had no intention of getting married to anyone anytime soon.

A half an hour later, Eva and Luke drove away from the barn in a horse-drawn cart covered in flowers. Viv Shuster had passed out bubble wands and plastic jars of soap and water, along with paper cones of dried lavender for everyone to blow and throw as the bride and groom rode away.

They weren't really going anywhere. The flower-covered cart only disappeared around the far side of the farmhouse. Eva and Luke would spend their wedding night in their own bed and leave for their honeymoon on Monday.

The party continued. There was more dancing and horsing around. Derek kept up his front pretty well, he thought. He and Amy hung out and joined in the fun.

Around two, as things were kind of winding down, Amy leaned in close. "Let me grab a few things from the house and I'll follow you to the ranch."

One more night.

He really wanted that.

But if he got it, he just knew he'd make a damn fool of himself in the morning. When she told him she was leaving, he would beg her to stay. Bad enough she was going. No reason to embarrass himself when she left.

"Listen," he said.

She gazed up at him through those innocent eyes. "Yeah?"

"Not here."

"Um. Okay…"

He grabbed her hand and started walking away from the party, out of the glow of the strings of lights, out of sight of the remaining guests.

"Derek?" She sounded confused, like she didn't have any idea what the hell was going on. He just pulled her farther on, back to the hackberry tree and the deep shadows provided by its leafy branches.

Once they were sheltered from any prying eyes, he let go of her hand and stepped away.

"Derek, what is going on?"

He rubbed the back of his neck which was suddenly stiff and aching. "Look. We don't need to drag this out, do we?"

Her face was only a shadow, but her big eyes got bigger. "I don't understand what you're—"

"What I mean is, I had a great time these last couple of weeks with you. The best time. You're beautiful and sexy and just about perfect and it's meant a lot to me, that we could spend this time together, kind of put the past behind us. I think we've done that. I really do. I also think it's better if we just call this over now."

"Over?" Those eyes shone so bright. "But I thought we were together. I thought we might—"

"Uh-uh." He couldn't stand to hear her say those things. He couldn't let himself *believe* those things, couldn't get his hopes up that if he let her keep talking, she might tell him what he longed to hear. That wasn't going to happen. He wasn't that kind of guy. "No. You have a life. I have a life. It's not going to work and it's better if we just face that now."

"Derek, please…" She reached for him.

"Don't." Hands up, he backed off another step. "I don't want to hear it, okay? I don't need to hear it. I just need to get going."

"But I thought that we understood each other. I thought we wanted the same things. I want to *be* with you." She reached for him again. "I want to—"

"Knock it off." He pushed her hand away. "I mean it. I don't know what you're talking about. I just want to wish you well and say goodbye."

Her face changed. Even in the darkness he could see it. Her eyes gleamed with tears, but they were furious tears. "Derek Dalton, this is such crap. You've been freaking out all night and you really need to stop that. You're acting like a coward. I don't believe you're doing this. I don't believe you actually think you're going to—"

"Enough." He cut her off again. "I can't take this anymore. I'm leaving now and that's how I want it, that's who I am."

"But we—"

"Goodbye, Amy. Have a great life."

And he turned and started walking fast, out from under the branches of the tree, straight for his pickup parked along the winding dirt driveway on the far side of the house.

Did she follow? He had no idea. Because he never once looked back.

Chapter 11

Amy stood alone in the dark under the spreading branches of the big, old tree and felt her heart breaking all over again.

How could this be happening? It was just like thirteen years ago.

She considered going after him, begging him to reconsider.

But he didn't want her following him. He'd made that more than clear.

He didn't want her, period.

She'd been living in a fool's dream. He didn't feel the way that she did. It had all just been a fling to him.

The man had crushed her heart to bits all over again.

What to do now?

No way could she return to the remains of the party.

Her arms wrapped around herself, shoulders hunched, eyes squinted hard to keep from letting the tears fall, she ducked out from under the tree and made for the house.

She got all the way across the dark yard, up the steps and inside without meeting a single soul. The house was quiet. She dropped to the straight chair in the foyer to tug off her boots. Then, on stocking feet, she ran up the stairs to her room and quietly shut the door. Leaning back against it, she let go of the boots.

They thudded to the floor. The sound of them dropping finished her somehow. She broke.

Her knees buckled. She slid down the door, buried her head in her hands and let the tears fall.

How long did she crouch there, knees drawn up under her chin, crying like a silly twit for a guy who didn't want her?

Way too long.

Finally, on shaky legs, she pushed herself

upright again. She should wash her face, brush her teeth.

But she had no energy for any of that. Instead, she peeled off her maid-of-honor dress and fell across the bed in her lacy underwear.

She tried to sleep. Maybe she did sleep a little, dropping off exhausted. But then she jolted awake to remember that it had all gone bad and she could only stare at the far wall through another bout of sheer misery. She couldn't wait for daylight when she could pack up her stuff, throw it all in her Audi and get out of town.

At the crack of dawn, she snuck down the hall for a quick shower and to finally brush her teeth. Back in her room again, she packed like a madwoman, only pausing to wipe away the damn tears that wouldn't stop falling.

In fifteen minutes flat, she was ready to go. Her crammed-full suitcases waited against the wall. Her computer equipment was unplugged, unhooked and disassembled, stacked beside her bags. As she glared at it all and tried to decide what to haul downstairs first, someone tapped on the door.

"Amy?" Mikayla. "Eva's got breakfast ready downstairs."

Amy stood frozen. If she opened the damn door, Mikayla would see it all—her red, runny nose and bloodshot eyes, the stupid tears that kept spilling over and dribbling down her blotchy face.

Mikayla rapped on the door again. "Amy, are you in there?"

"I'm here," she gave out reluctantly. Her voice sounded like a couple of pieces of coarse sandpaper rubbing together.

"Amy, what's going on?" The real concern in Mikayla's tone had the tear factory going great guns all over again. "Why didn't you go to Derek's for the night?"

She yanked the door wide. "Don't mention that name." She glowered at the woman she'd begun to think of as a friend.

Mikayla's pretty face scrunched up with sympathy and concern. "Aw, honey. What's happened?" She held out her arms.

That did it. Amy threw herself against Mikayla's big belly and sobbed out brokenly, "Derek ended it. I thought we were together. But, he called it off with me. I left some of my stuff at his house and I still have his key and I don't even have the energy to go over there, get my things and throw the key in his face. Everything is… I don't know how to even tell you. It's awful. Terrible. So much worse than bad…"

"Oh, sweetie. Oh, hon…" Mikayla stroked

her back, ran her hands down Amy's arms. "Whatever it is, you'll work it out. It'll be okay."

"No, it won't. It never will. He hurt me so bad. He did it again, because, you know, I guess once just wasn't enough."

Mikayla took her by the shoulders and guided her backwards to the bed. "Sit down." Amy obeyed. Grabbing the box of tissues on the nightstand, Mikayla took Amy's hand. She plunked the tissues in it. "Blow your nose and stay right there. I mean it. Do. Not. Move."

"Fine," she replied—except it came out "Fide" because she really did need the tissues.

Mikayla took off through the door. Amy heard her footsteps going down the stairs.

Two minutes later, Mikayla was back, this time with Eva. They hovered in the doorway.

"Amy, what's happened?" Eva cried, which only caused Amy to burst into tears all over again.

The two women flew to her side. They sat on the bed, Eva on her right and Mikayla on her left, and wrapped their arms around her while she cried some more.

At least that storm of weeping didn't last long. "I think I'm pretty close to cried out," she confessed after blowing her nose for about the hundredth time.

"Talk," ordered Eva. "Tell us everything so we can help."

Amy looked from one dear, concerned face to the other. All these years and years she'd told no one what had happened the summer she was eighteen.

And look how well that had gone.

Not well at all.

So, she blew her nose one more time and she did what Eva demanded. She talked.

She told them everything, about the past, the baby that maybe wasn't, about the wedding at the courthouse, about how true Derek had been to her, right there for her when she needed him most, about the cheap motel and the trucks going by on the highway. About how it all ended, about how she came back nine years ago to talk to him and he came to CU to find her, but neither of them knew the other had tried to reach out.

About how it all started up again when she came back for the wedding, about how she'd really believed they would make it this time. How she'd made arrangements with her boss so she could live right here in Rust Creek Falls, how she'd braced her father and he'd ended up admitting that he believed Derek really did love her, that her dad had wished her happiness with the man she'd never stopped loving.

And then how, last night, Derek had broken her heart all over again.

"He doesn't want me. He doesn't love me. He told me he had a great time the last couple of weeks. He said to have a nice life and he left me under that big tree between the house and the barn." Amy gave one last sniffle and wiped her nose.

Eva asked gently, "Is that it? Is that all?"

"Isn't that enough?" Amy cried.

And Mikayla said, "Well, there's just one little problem..."

Amy slid her a suspicious glance. "What?" she grumbled.

Mikayla wrapped an arm around her. "Well, honey. The problem is that you've got it all wrong."

Amy sputtered in outrage, but before she could argue, Eva backed Mikayla. "She's right, Amy. Derek loves you."

"No, he—"

"Yes." Eva sat tall and spoke firmly. "His love is written all over his face every time he looks at you."

Mikayla took Amy's hand and put it on the round crest of her own belly where her unborn baby slept. "A man who stands by you, who makes you know that you're wanted when things get rough... A man like that is worth fighting for. And he did stand by you, way back when. He was there when you needed him the most. Try looking at it from his point of view, why don't you? Your father finally told you what really happened. Derek stepped aside so that you could have the education you'd worked so hard for."

Amy gulped and nodded. "I know. I realize now that he did what he did then for me and that I was too hurt and confused to see it at the time."

"Kind of like now?" Eva suggested gently.

"No!" Amy argued. "It's not like now—okay, yeah. I'm hurt and confused now, but I *told* him I don't want to go. I told him I want to stay, to be with him."

"That's lame," Mikayla said.

"Lame!" Amy practically shouted.

Mikayla didn't even flinch. "Yeah, lame. If you want to make it work this time, I think you're going to have to say right out loud that you love him and that you're ready now to stand by him like he once stood by you. You have to be strong and you have to be clear. You have to know in your heart that what you had with him—what you *could* have again if you don't give up now—is what matters most. Love. That's what you had and that's what you still have. Just don't quit on love. Because a guy who steps up, that's a guy worth fighting for."

Eva asked, "Last night, did you tell him in so many words that you love him? Did you say that you want to stay here in town, that you've talked to your boss and you can work right here and still keep your job?"

"I never got a chance. He didn't let me."

"Make the chance," Mikayla and Eva insisted in unison.

"But what if he just says no to me again?"

"Then you'll know for sure," replied Mikayla.

Deep down, Amy did understand what her friends were trying to tell her, but the brokenhearted, scared little girl inside her just had to ask, "I'll know what for sure?"

"That you gave him your all. You gave your love every possible chance. If you go all the way and he still turns you down, at least you'll always know that this time you did everything you could to make it work."

Eva's hand, light as a breath, stroked Amy's hair. "We know you're scared. You wouldn't be human if you weren't. It's okay to be scared.

What's not okay is to give up without first giving love everything you've got."

"I just…what if I'm only asking for more heartache?"

Mikayla snort-laughed. "Have you seen yourself? You're about at max heartache now. Giving your all is only going to make you stronger."

Was it? Really?

Amy had serious doubts on that score.

And yet, she knew the truth when she heard it. Her friends were right. She hadn't gone all the way last night, hadn't really put her heart right out there. She'd failed to declare her love out loud.

She needed to do that, once and for all.

If she didn't, she would never know if, just maybe, they could have made it work.

"Okay," she said to no one in particular as she jumped to her feet.

The two women on the bed stared up at her. "Okay, what?" demanded Mikayla.

"Okay, I'm going for it."

"Yes!" Eva shoved both fists high in the air as Mikayla muttered, "Finally."

Amy strode to the foot of the bed. From there, she paced back and forth. "Chances are he's at the ranch. But no matter where he is, he'll have to go home eventually. When he gets there, I'll be waiting for him and I'll pull out all the stops this time to get through to him."

Eva got up and came to her. With a cry, Amy grabbed for her friend. And then Mikayla was there, too. The three of them held each other good and tight.

"All right then," Amy said at last as the other two stepped back. She smoothed her hair and straightened her shirt. "I know I look like I cried all night."

"You look beautiful," said Eva.

"Not true. But I'll take it. Wish me luck."

"We wish you love," said Mikayla. "Because that's what matters most."

They walked her downstairs. She hugged them once more at the door and went out alone—and got only as far as the top step that led down to the yard and her dusty Audi waiting in the morning sun.

She stopped when she heard a truck approaching. The sun was wicked bright, so she brought her hand up to shade her poor, tired eyes.

And she saw Derek's red pickup barreling along the driveway, coming right for her, kicking up a big plume of dust in its wake.

She stood there with her mouth hanging open as he skidded to a stop at the base of the steps. He flung his door wide and jumped out.

"Amy," he said, his mouth grim and his jaw set. He strode up the stairs to her.

Oh, had any man ever looked so handsome, in good jeans and dress boots, a tan plaid shirt and a fine, gray hat?

"Amy." He swept off his hat, tossed it over his shoulder and dropped to his knees. "Amy, I love you."

Was he really here, kneeling before her? "Derek?" she asked, her voice barely a whisper, half-fearing she might be hallucinating from exhaustion and a long night's worth of brokenhearted misery and crying jags.

He put a hand to his heart. "Amy, I was a pure coward yesterday and I didn't sleep a wink all night. I've just been afraid, that's all. Afraid that I was living in a fool's dream, afraid that if I asked you to stay or offered to come live in Boulder with you, all I'd get was a flat no. I was so sure I was only going to end up losing you all over again. So, I went and beat you to the losing part. I said goodbye before you could. I told you it was over.

"Because I'm an idiot who tried to escape getting his heart broken by walking away first.

An idiot who spent the rest of last night realizing that all I'd accomplished was the breaking of my own damn heart. So yeah. I'm an idiot, but I'm *your* idiot, Amy. If only you'll have me."

Her throat was clutching, more tears rising—but this time in the good way. This time with joy. "Yes! Yes, I will have you and love you and be yours. It's all I ever wanted, Derek Dalton. I love you, too. And I want to move here, to Rust Creek Falls, where I've always dreamed I might someday make a home again. I want to move here and be with you—which reminds me, I failed to mention that I've got that all arranged. I talked to my bosses and they agreed I can make the move to Rust Creek Falls and still keep my job. And I talked to my dad and he admitted what he did, how he begged you to let me go that summer we got married, how he convinced you that my being with you would hold me back. He also said he'd had a feeling we would get back together and he was glad for us.

"Derek, I should have told you last night. I should have stood up and fought to make you see that I really do love you and want to be with you, only you. And I was coming to see you, just now, when you drove up, coming to tell you I want to move into your house on the Circle D with you. I want to love you and take care of you and have you take care of me and I want to do that for the rest of our lives."

He gazed up at her, his gorgeous, messy hair flopping over his forehead, pure love in those incomparable green eyes of his. How could she not have seen it before? How could she not have known that he was hers if only she would reach out and claim him? "Wait!" he said with teasing urgency.

"What?" she asked, alarmed.

"Amy Wainwright, did you just tell me yes?"

"Derek, *yes*." A goofy trill of laughter escaped her. "Yes, I said yes." He pulled something from his pocket, something that shone so bright. She gasped. "Derek, is that…"

"Amy." He reached out. "Will you give me your hand?"

"Yes." She giggled again. "Somehow, I can't stop saying yes." He slipped the ring on her finger. It was perfect, with a large central diamond in a halo of smaller stones. "Oh, Derek. It's just beautiful."

He looked so earnest, staring up at her. "If you'd rather make the choice yourself—"

"No way. It's mine and I'm keeping it. I love it." She wrapped her other hand around it and brought both hands against her heart just as he swept upward to his full height. She swayed toward him.

"Amy. My love." He gathered her close as she lifted her face to him. "I have a powerful feeling we're going to make it this time."

"Oh, Derek. Yes. Yes, we will make it. You and me and the rest of our lives. A home on the Circle D with you, and children, I hope. That's what I want, Derek. That's what we will have."

He bent close and his lips touched hers. She surged onto her toes then, sliding her hands up over his broad shoulders to clasp them around his neck.

The kiss was long and slow and deep, sealing their promise, each to the other.

When she dropped back to her heels again and opened her eyes, he said, "I gave up on us twice, Amy—thirteen years ago and then last night. I'm done giving up. This time, it's forever. I will never walk away again."

She stroked the hair at his temple, traced the shape of his ear. "Good. Because I'm sticking with you now, no matter what. You are mine, Derek Dalton, and I am never letting you go."

"That reminds me…" He reached in his breast pocket a second time, bringing out a thin gold chain with another ring at the end of it, a ring with a gold-tone band and a square-cut imitation diamond.

She let out a cry. "Oh, Derek. You kept it. You kept my ring for all these years." She waved her hand in front of her face. "Now, just look at me, crying all over again."

"Turn around," he instructed. Dashing away the pesky tears, she turned and lifted her hair off her neck so he could hook the clasp. "There," he said. His warm lips brushed her nape.

She curled her fingers protectively over the old ring with her left hand, cherishing the feel of it, as her new ring glittered in the morning light. "So it was never lost, after all." She turned to him again. "Thank you."

He tipped up her chin and kissed her—first, her tear-wet cheeks and then her lips, a chaste kiss, infinitely sweet. As he lifted his head, she heard a sound from the house.

"Don't look now," she warned, "but I think we have an audience."

The door was open just a crack. A grinning Eva pulled it wide. Behind her stood Luke, Mikayla and Bailey, too.

"About time," muttered Luke.

"Congratulations," said Eva. "Love wins out. It always does."

Mikayla started clapping, causing the other three to follow suit.

Derek laughed, put his arm around Amy's shoulders and pulled her close to his side. "She said yes," he announced proudly. "She's going to marry me—again."

"I'm so glad," Mikayla said.

"Again?" Bailey grumbled. "I'll bet *that's* a good story. And didn't I tell you last night that you guys were fooling no one with your friends-only act?"

"Come on inside, you two." Luke swept out a hand toward the house. "Eva's got breakfast on."

"French toast stuffed with cream cheese and blackberry jam," Eva tempted them. "With whipped cream on top and your choice of syrup—oh, and hickory smoked bacon, because what's a decadent after-wedding breakfast without a little bacon?"

"You're on," said Derek. "But give us a minute, okay? We'll be right in."

When Eva shut the door, Derek tugged Amy close again for another lovely, lengthy kiss. "Does it get any better than this?" he asked at last.

She beamed up at him. "I don't see how it can, but I know that it will. Because we're together now, for real. And I do honestly believe in us now. I know in my deepest heart that at last we are strong together, you and me, Derek. And I also know that through the years, we will only get stronger."

He bent close and whispered, "I love you, Amy Wainwright, and that means forever. From this day forward, nothing and no one can tear us apart."

A few minutes later, they went inside together, into Eva's warm, busy kitchen, hand in hand.

Mikayla asked to see the ring and Amy proudly held out her hand.

Eva left the stove to have a look. "Just beautiful," she said.

"Gorgeous," Mikayla agreed.

Luke got up to clap Derek on the back. "Way to go, man."

Then Eva waved a pot holder. "Sit down, you two. Your breakfast is ready."

Derek pulled out Amy's chair for her, stealing a quick kiss as she took her seat. He sat beside her.

"Two more damn love birds," Bailey complained. "Everyone in this town's gone love-crazy, and that's a plain fact."

"It's Rust Creek Falls," said Eva, as if that explained everything.

Mikayla laughed. "Watch out, Bailey. You'll be next."

Scowling, he muttered, "Never again."

Amy brushed Derek's arm under the table. He turned his hand over and she twined her fingers with his.

It was a moment she would treasure forever: a bright, summer morning at Sunshine Farm with good friends around her, the love of her life right here beside her, her hand in his. This was true happiness.

After too many long, lonely years away, Amy Wainwright had come home at last.

* * * * *

Get 4 FREE REWARDS!

We'll send you 2 FREE Books plus 2 FREE Mystery Gifts.

FREE
Value Over
$20

Both the **Harlequin® Special Edition** and **Harlequin® Heartwarming™** series feature compelling novels filled with stories of love and strength where the bonds of friendship, family and community unite.

Get 4 FREE REWARDS!

We'll send you 2 FREE Books <u>plus</u> 2 FREE Mystery Gifts.

FREE Value Over **$20**

Both the **Harlequin® Historical** and **Harlequin® Romance** series feature compelling novels filled with emotion and simmering romance.

Get 4 FREE REWARDS!

We'll send you 2 FREE Books <u>plus</u> 2 FREE Mystery Gifts.

FREE Value Over **$20**

Both the **Romance** and **Suspense** collections feature compelling novels written by many of today's bestselling authors.

YES! Please send me 2 FREE novels from the Essential Romance or Essential Suspense Collection and my 2 FREE gifts (gifts are worth about $10 retail). After receiving them, if I don't wish to receive any more books, I can return the shipping statement marked "cancel." If I don't cancel, I will receive 4 brand-new novels every month and be billed just $7.24 each in the U.S. or $7.49 each in Canada. That's a savings of up to 38% off the cover price. It's quite a bargain! Shipping and handling is just 50¢ per book in the U.S. and $1.25 per book in Canada.* I understand that accepting the 2 free books and gifts places me under no obligation to buy anything. I can always return a shipment and cancel at any time by calling the number below. The free books and gifts are mine to keep no matter what I decide.

Choose one: ☐ **Essential Romance**   ☐ **Essential Suspense**
(194/394 MDN GQ6M)   (191/391 MDN GQ6M)

Name (please print)

Address   Apt. #

City   State/Province   Zip/Postal Code

Email: Please check this box ☐ if you would like to receive newsletters and promotional emails from Harlequin Enterprises ULC and its affiliates. You can unsubscribe anytime.

Mail to the **Harlequin Reader Service:**
IN U.S.A.: P.O. Box 1341, Buffalo, NY 14240-8531
IN CANADA: P.O. Box 603, Fort Erie, Ontario L2A 5X3

Want to try 2 free books from another series! Call 1-800-873-8635 or visit www.ReaderService.com.

*Terms and prices subject to change without notice. Prices do not include sales taxes, which will be charged (if applicable) based on your state or country of residence. Canadian residents will be charged applicable taxes. Offer not valid in Quebec. This offer is limited to one order per household. Books received may not be as shown. Not valid for current subscribers to the Essential Romance or Essential Suspense Collection. All orders subject to approval. Credit or debit balances in a customer's account(s) may be offset by any other outstanding balance owed by or to the customer. Please allow 4 to 6 weeks for delivery. Offer available while quantities last.

Your Privacy—Your information is being collected by Harlequin Enterprises ULC, operating as Harlequin Reader Service. For a complete summary of the information we collect, how we use this information and to whom it is disclosed, please visit our privacy notice located at corporate.harlequin.com/privacy-notice. From time to time we may also exchange your personal information with reputable third parties. If you wish to opt out of this sharing of your personal information, please visit readerservice.com/consumerschoice or call 1-800-873-8635. **Notice to California Residents**—Under California law, you have specific rights to control and access your data. For more information on these rights and how to exercise them, visit corporate.harlequin.com/california-privacy.

STRS22R2